Promises Made...

Promises Made...

SAMANTHA DUPREE

Promises Made…

Samantha Dupree

FIRST EDITION

ISBN: 978-1-7355039-3-6 (hardcover)
ISBN: 978-1-7355039-4-3 (paperback)
ISBN: 978-1-7355039-5-0 (ebook)

Library of Congress Control Number: 2021924962

MH
Morrison House

Contents

The author wishes to express her appreciation to her very talented friend, Kari Shipley, who graciously agreed to paint the covers of *Secrets Behind the Hedges, Promises Made…*, and *Live, Love, Be…* Kari resides in Delray Beach, Florida, and all funds from her work go directly to *CommunityGreening.org*

Prologue

Midnight, June 16th, 2015.

Liv was curled up in her bed in the fetal position, hugging her pillow and crying. William slowly cracked her bedroom door open.

"Mom, are you awake? I'm home." Liv sat up and William gave his mother a warm hug and then sat on her bed.

"William, I'm so glad you're home. I don't understand what your father is doing. How do you just decide all of a sudden that you don't want to be a husband and a father anymore after twenty years of marriage?"

"I don't know, Mom."

"William, I think I've been a pretty good wife and mother over the years. Now, I do realize me getting sick was rough on everyone, but we took vows and we made promises. Doesn't that mean anything? Okay, so he doesn't want to be married to me anymore, but after twenty years together, wouldn't you have the common decency to sit down and have a conversation with your wife? Why, William? Why did he do this? Not just to me, but to all of us?"

William hugged her again. "Mom, let's face it, Dad has been acting differently for quite some time now. And by the way, just so you know, I'm not a kid anymore. Mom, I've noticed his excessive drinking, his new tattoos, and Dad's obsession with country music concerts. It's all super weird. And I also know he's been sleeping in the guest room for a while now."

"William, do you think there's someone else?"

"To be honest with you, Mom, it really wouldn't surprise me."

"Well, William, I can tell you this. I've been faithful to that man for twenty years."

"Listen, Mom, I think you need to get some sleep."

"William, I really don't think that I can. I'm scared of what's going to happen to all of us."

"Don't worry, Mom. We're going to figure this all out. I'll stay here with you until you fall asleep."

"Okay," said Liv as she lay down.

William tucked his mother in and slept in a chair by her side all night.

The next morning, Liv was in Abby Goldstein's waiting room with her mother by her side. Mrs. Goldstein's secretary opened the office door and said, "Mrs. Donovan, if you'll please follow me, Mrs. Goldstein is ready for you."

Liv and her mother followed the secretary into the conference room where five people sat around a large conference table.

"Good morning, Mrs. Donovan. I'm Abby Goldstein and this is your legal team." Mrs. Goldstein introduced Liv to two paralegals and two forensic accountants. "First of all, I just want to start out by saying that everyone around this table is very sorry that this has happened to you and your family. We all know divorce is never easy."

"But here's the thing," said Liv. "I don't want to get divorced. I think a trial separation would be a good place to start and then we can go from there."

Mrs. Goldstein put her elbows on the table and folded her hands. "Mrs. Donovan, I think you're a tad bit confused. You don't have a choice in this matter. Your husband has filed for divorce. We also found out that he hired his divorce attorney a year-and-a-half ago. So, you see, he's been planning this for some time. Mrs. Donovan, I've been doing this for over thirty years and the fact that he took all of the money out of the bank accounts is not a good sign. That's why I asked Mr. Kellogg and his partner to join us today. They are the best forensic accountants money can buy. Mr. Kellogg is also a former FBI agent, so, you see, you're in very good hands."

"I'm sorry. I don't understand," said Liv.

"May I call you Olivia?"

"Of course."

"Olivia, in my experience, men like your husband tend to hide their assets when they're going through a divorce."

"What do you mean?"

"How much money would you say your husband has been making the last five years?"

"If I had to guess, I'd say close to a million dollars a year."

"Well, I can assure you that he's not going to want to give you close to what you deserve as far as child support and alimony. Mr. Kellogg is going to make sure you get what you deserve. Now, did you bring all of your jewelry?"

"Yes," Liv said as she pulled her jewelry box out of a large tote bag.

"Helen," said Mrs. Goldstein, "can you please take pictures of all of the pieces and put them into our safe? Now, Olivia, did your husband give you all of these items?"

"Actually, no."

"Well the pieces he did not give you can go back home with you. And what about the jewelry you're wearing?"

Liv looked down at the ring Kurt had just given her. "He actually just gave me this for our twentieth anniversary two days ago."

"Unfortunately, that will have to go into the safe as well."

Liv slowly slid the ring off of her finger. Tears began running down her face. Mrs. Goldstein handed her a box of tissues. "I'm sorry," said Liv. "I just can't believe this is happening."

Liv's mom put her arm around her daughter. "I think she's just in shock," she said, turning toward Mrs. Goldstein. "And her health has not been the best these past few years." Then she explained all about Liv's medical condition.

"Well, excuse me for saying this," Mrs. Goldstein exclaimed, "but what a bastard! I've seen some horrible men over the years, but I think your soon-to-be ex-husband takes the cake. But don't you worry. I promise you, you're in good hands. So before we end the meeting, I'm going to need you to sign the retainer page, and I will also need a check."

Liv looked down at the signature page. The retainer was $25,000. "I'm sorry, but I really can't sign this. Remember, he drained all of our bank accounts."

Liv's mom took out her checkbook. "I got this," she said, as she filled out the check. "Now, Mrs. Goldstein, make sure you protect my daughter and nail this asshole to the wall. I'm sorry, Liv, but what he has done to you and the children is unforgivable!"

The next two weeks were a whirlwind. Liv finally got a credit card and her mother took her to a local bank to open up accounts for herself and the children. The Gallagher family all decided to pitch in, giving Liv a loan of a little over $500,000 so she wouldn't have to worry and the kids' lives could remain the same, at least for the time being.

After two weeks, there was still no word from Kurt. And as if Liv didn't already have enough on her plate, the charity's first golf event for POTS research was taking place in less than a month. The event planner had begged her to cancel, but Liv refused. "I will not allow him to ruin this event," she declared. "There are too many people counting on me. I have over a hundred golfers signed up. Not to mention the fact that Dr. Grubb is flying in with his colleagues from the University of Toledo Medical Center. No, this event must, and will, go on as planned."

Now the only thing left to do was to find a new sponsor for the event. Kurt's company, Eagle Armor, had been the original sponsor, but no more. Luckily, David Santoro had stepped in to save the day with his company, the Ramshead Restaurant Group, as the new sponsor. He had come back into Liv's life and was, once again, right by her side.

As for Liv, she went quickly from being heartbroken to being incredibly pissed off. The only sadness she felt was when she looked at her beautiful children. She found herself wondering if she had what it would take to be both the mother and father to all four of them. She remembered something that her grandmother always told her: *Family first.* In the days to come, Olivia would cling to her grandmother's words like a life preserver, hoping that they would help her through the rough seas ahead. And at the end of the day, Olivia Whittaker knew that life must, and will, go on…

CHAPTER 1

Chase Winston Montgomery IV

Over the next few weeks, Liv spent many sleepless nights staring at her bedroom ceiling and endless hours crying. She had absolutely no appetite and had lost nearly fifteen pounds at this point. Ms. Dee, her beloved housekeeper and nanny, kept saying, "Ms. Olivia, you really need to eat something. You're wasting away to nothing!"

Liv's reply was always the same. "Ms. Dee, Apparently crying burns a lot of calories."

On Friday, June 24th, Liv was sitting at the kitchen table drinking her morning coffee when Austin came flying into the kitchen.

"Good morning, Ma."

"Austin, are you running late for work again?" That summer, all three of Liv's sons were working at The Breakers Hotel. Austin was working over at the golf course as a caddy, William as an outdoor bartender, and Jeffrey as a cabana attendant.

"Don't worry, Mom. I won't be late. I just wanted to ask you a quick question before I head out."

"Okay, son, what's on your mind?" Austin was Liv's oldest son. Tragically, his biological parents had lost their battle with drugs and alcohol several years ago. After their untimely passing, Liv and Kurt had stepped in and legally adopted him at the age of twelve. Since then, he had blended seamlessly into their family, and, during these last few weeks, had become Liv's rock.

"Well, here's the deal, Mom. We're all super worried about you."

"I understand that, Austin, but you have to realize that I really am trying my best."

"I know you are, Mom, and I get that you're extremely upset. But here's the million-dollar question I have for you: after everything that Dad has done to you and to the rest of us, do you really want him back?"

"Hell, no. That man is out of my life forever."

"Okay, so what's all the crying about then?"

"I don't know, Austin. I just feel scared." (Liv was overwhelmed with worry about her uncertain financial future and with her new role as a single parent.)

"Well, Mom, I think you really need to snap out of this funk that you're in."

"Austin, I'm not disagreeing with you, but do you have any suggestions for your mother?"

"As a matter of fact, I do. I want us to go over to the club tonight, for the Friday night buffet. Mom, I think it would do you a world of good to get out of the house for the evening."

"You're sweet, son, but I really don't see that happening."

"Why not, Mom?"

"Austin, I don't think you realize how many phone calls and text messages I've received since your father's disappearing act. Son, To put it simply, I know I'm the talk of the town at the moment."

"Mom, who cares?! And, besides, do you really think you're the only woman in Palm Beach that's ever gotten divorced? Come on, Mom. This island was built on scandals."

Liv poured some more coffee into her cup and stirred in some cream. "So, will William, Jeffrey, and Rose be joining us for dinner as well?"

"No, Mom, unfortunately, William and Jeffrey have to work late tonight, and I already asked Ms. Dee to babysit for Rose, so it would just be you and me."

"What time did you want to go?" asked Liv.

"Well, I called over to the club yesterday and I got us a seven o'clock reservation."

Liv sighed and finally gave in. "Okay, son, you win. I'll be ready to leave at 6:45."

"Great!" Austin ran across the kitchen and gave his mother a big hug.

"Have a good day at work, son," said Liv.

"I will. And Mom, don't worry about tonight. I know we're going to have a great time!" And with that, Austin ran out the back door.

That evening when Austin and Liv walked through the main dining room of the Palm Beach Bath and Tennis Club and out onto the patio, Liv felt as though all eyes were on her. The hostess escorted them over to a lovely table with a beautiful view of the ocean. And then, Liv's favorite waiter hurried over to take their drink orders.

"Good evening, Mrs. Donovan. Aren't you looking very pretty tonight," the waiter said.

"Thank you, Wade," replied Liv.

"Mrs. Donovan, I also wanted to take this opportunity to tell you how sorry I was to hear about you and Mr. Donovan."

Liv took a large gulp of her ice water. "That's very kind of you, Wade. So tell me, does everyone at the club know about my upcoming divorce?"

"Well, yes. It was brought up in our Monday morning staff meeting."

Great, thought Liv. *Just great.*

As Wade left to get their drinks, the manager of the club came by the table and put his hand on Liv's shoulder. "Olivia, I just wanted to come over and tell you how sorry I am."

"Thank you, Mr. Callaghan. And if you don't mind me asking, how did you find out?"

"Oh, I thought you knew. Kurt called me about a month ago and told me that the two of you were getting divorced. He also instructed me to put the club's membership solely in your name. But, obviously, that's a decision the board will have to make."

"Wait a minute, let me get this straight. Kurt called you a *month* ago?"

"Yes."

"Wow, this is unbelievable. So you knew I was getting divorced before I did."

As Wade returned with their drinks, Mr. Callaghan politely excused himself, saying, "Olivia, I truly am very sorry. And if there's anything I can do, please don't hesitate to ask."

Austin stood up and shook his hand. "Thank you, Mr. Callaghan. My family and I really do appreciate that."

"Of course. And I hope you both enjoy tonight's buffet."

Liv turned to Austin and said, "Austin, this is crazy. Your father told the manager of our beach club that he was leaving before he told his own wife!"

"Mom, please try to calm down. I really want us to try and have a nice dinner. Okay?"

"Okay, Austin, I'm sorry." Liv took a big sip of her Chardonnay and tried to calm her nerves.

"So, Mom, can we please go up to the buffet now? I'm starving."

"Sure, Austin, but before we go up, isn't that Chase Montgomery sitting behind you, two tables down?"

Austin turned around slowly. "Oh, wow, Mom! It sure is."

"Austin, I don't understand. I thought he was up in Atlanta working for Morgan Stanley."

"He was, but I guess I forgot to tell you—Morgan just transferred him back down here to their Palm Beach office. And when I spoke to him earlier in the week, he told me that he would be moving back home on Sunday."

"Well, that's wonderful news, Austin. I know how close you two have always been."

"Yeah, Chase has always been like a big brother to me and it's going to be great to have him back in town. Hey, Mom, before we hit the buffet, I'm going to go over and say hi to him and his family real quick, okay?"

"Of course, Austin. Take your time."

Austin rose and walked over to Chase's table. He hugged Chase and his parents. They chatted for a few moments and then they all got up and came over to Liv's table.

Liv stood up and said, "Well, hello, Montgomery family. It's so nice to see all of you again."

"Nice to see you, too, Mrs. Donovan," Chase replied.

Arthur Montgomery extended his hand and smiled warmly. "It's so good to see you, Olivia."

"Thank you, Arthur. You as well."

"Olivia, I have to say I was shocked to hear about your divorce," said Birdie Montgomery. "And I'm sure this whole mess must be terribly embarrassing for you. Luckily, nothing like that has ever happened in our family. Oh, and I imagine you're worried sick over your club membership, you poor dear."

"My membership?"

"Why, yes, Olivia, aren't you aware that after a divorce, no woman has ever kept her membership at the club? It just doesn't work that way around here, dear," she whispered.

Liv stood looking blankly at Birdie, unsure of how to respond, but then Birdie grabbed her husband's elbow and said, "Arthur, there's Karen Dougherty over at the tiki bar. I really must speak to her about this year's upcoming home tour event for the historical society. Please excuse us. Let's go, Arthur."

She turned and pulled Arthur away who glanced back and smiled once more at Liv. "Very nice to see you again, Olivia."

Liv nodded and managed a smile back.

"So, Chase," said Austin, "I didn't think you were coming back into town until Sunday."

"I wasn't, but the U-Haul was all packed and ready to go, so I decided to head home early."

"Well, it's great to have you back in town, man."

"Brother, I must say, it feels amazing to be back."

"So, you're going to be staying at your parents' house?"

"Yep. In their guest house."

"Mom," said Austin, "didn't you go to the Montgomery's house last year when it was on the historical society's home tour?"

"Oh, yes," said Liv, "it's a darling home. I adore its wraparound porch and black-and-white-striped awnings."

"Thanks," said Chase. "It's a great house, and it's been in our family for generations. And the guest house will be perfect for me until I can find a place of my own." Then, turning to Austin, he said, "Austin, we're still golfing this week, right?"

"You bet. I booked us a one o'clock tee time on Wednesday."

"Perfect. I can't wait. Oh, and by the way, Mrs. Donovan, I'm really looking forward to your golf event."

"Chase," said Liv, "I'm sorry, I didn't realize that you were playing."

"Austin didn't tell you? My father's firm bought a foursome last week."

"Oh, that's wonderful, Chase. And please tell your father I said thank you."

"I will. But before you head over to the buffet, do you think I could speak to you alone for a moment?"

"Of course. Austin, you go on ahead and I'll meet you back at the table."

"Sure thing, Mom."

Liv and Chase strolled out onto the boardwalk, which led down toward the beach. "So, Mrs. Donovan—"

"Chase, please call me Liv."

"Okay, Liv. I just wanted to tell you how sorry I am for everything that you're going through."

"Thank you, Chase. I truly do appreciate you saying that."

"Also, as you probably already know, I think that you're an amazing woman. And to put it bluntly, in my opinion, you have literally saved Austin. I mean, let's face it, without you, I don't know where he'd be today."

"Oh, Chase, that's very kind of you. But I honestly feel that Austin and I have saved each other. He has been such an amazing blessing in my life and I thank God every day that he's a part of our family."

"So, I was thinking maybe after we finish golfing on Wednesday, I could bring some steaks over to the house and cookout for the family."

"Oh, Chase, that's a great idea and I know Austin would love that."

"Perfect. So let me get your phone number and I'll text you on Wednesday morning to confirm." Chase took out his phone and Liv recited her number.

"Chase, I'm so glad we ran into you tonight."

"Me, too."

Liv went through the buffet line and then returned to the table where she filled Austin in on her conversation with Chase.

"Mom, Chase is a great guy, and I'm so thankful that he's always been such a big part of my life. And I'm telling you, Mom, there's no doubt in my mind that he's sole the reason that I fell in love with the game of golf. So, Mom, now that we've had a nice dinner, what do you say we go grab a drink in town before we head home?"

"Austin, are you asking your mother to go to a bar?"

"You bet I am. It's time, Mom. Grab your purse and I'll have them pull the car around."

"Wait a minute, Austin. You do realize I haven't been to a bar in over twenty years."

"I know, but William just texted me and he wants us to meet him at HMF. C'mon, please?"

"Okay, I'll go, but for just one drink and then I'm heading home. And, son, just so you know, I'm only drinking water."

"Okay, Mom. Whatever makes you happy." And with that, he was off to get the car.

CHAPTER 2

Liv's Next Chapter

As Austin and Liv drove down South County road towards The Breakers Hotel, Liv started to become more and more anxious. "Austin, as you know, I've been to The Breakers many times, but I've actually never been to HMF. Isn't it a nightclub?"

"No, Mom, just relax. It's not a nightclub. It's more of an upscale lounge. And by the way, Mom, do you really think William and I would take you to some wild nightclub?"

I would certainly hope not, thought Liv.

As Austin pulled up in front of the valet stand, William walked over and opened his mother's door. "Hi, Mom," he said. "Are you ready to have some fun?"

Liv smiled and linked arms with William. As they strolled through The Breakers' Italian Renaissance-style lobby, Liv couldn't help but think back to the last time she was here. The words "a goodbye dinner" kept running through her head.

After they ascended the staircase to HMF, they were greeted by a beautiful young hostess who was wearing a short black dress, black high heels, and classic red lipstick. Her hair was pulled back into a tight bun which showed off her large diamond-stud earrings.

"Welcome to HMF," she said. "Would you like a table this evening, or are you heading over to the bar?"

"We're just going to find some seats at the bar," William replied. "But thanks." Then he turned to Austin. "Austin, do you see any of the guys?"

"No, but Beau just texted me. They're almost here."

"Boys, what's going on?" asked Liv.

"Well, Mom, this is your big night out, so we've invited some of our friends to join us."

Liv put her arms around her two sons as they walked toward the bar and said, "Austin and William, do you see that giant clock behind the bar?"

"Yes," the boys replied in unison.

"So here's the deal. Your mother is staying here for exactly one hour. When that clock strikes eleven, I'm heading home."

"Okay, Mom," said Austin. "Whatever you say."

"Great," said Liv, taking a seat on a large oversized leather bar stool. "Now, can one of you please order me a sparkling water with ice and lime?"

Austin waved down the bartender and ordered his mother's drink. Liv spun her barstool around and took in the room. That evening, the bar and lounge were packed with the beautiful people of Palm Beach, all of whom were dressed impeccably. Suddenly, Liv felt very out of place in her Lilly Pulitzer cocktail dress from a few seasons ago. When her sparkling water arrived, she sipped it through a cocktail straw while a thousand things went running through her head. She couldn't believe she was out at a bar. During her marriage to Kurt, she never went on girls' nights out. She didn't belong to book clubs or go away on girls' weekends, either. Liv had always believed that those things were nothing but trouble. So for the last twenty-one years, she had been at home with her husband and children.

William interrupted her thoughts. "Mom, some of our friends just got here," he said, waving them over to the bar. The next thing Liv knew, she was being introduced to a slew of people.

"Mom, this is Beau, his brother Ty, his other brother Tanner, and his youngest brother Dalton."

"Hi, Mrs. Donovan," said Beau. "It's great to finally meet you."

"Oh, please, call me Liv."

"Okay, Liv. I don't know if you're aware of this, but your sons have been coming down to my family's bar in Delray for years."

"Beau, you do realize that they both just turned twenty-one this year."

"Oh, don't worry. You have great kids. They just like listening to the live music. And chasing after the girls, if you know what I mean."

Oh, brother, thought Liv. She leaned over and whispered to Austin, "I need to use the ladies room. I'll be right back."

"No worries, Mom. I'll save your seat for you."

As Liv stood up, she glanced up at the clock, noticing that it was almost eleven. *Thank God*, she thought. *It's almost time for my exit.*

On her way back from the restroom, she couldn't help but notice a gorgeous man sitting at a high-top table near the bar. He had sandy blond hair, beautiful blue eyes, and was dressed perfectly. *He looks like he just stepped out of a Ralph Lauren catalog*, she thought. They made eye contact as she took her seat back at the bar. Just as Liv was about to tell her sons that she was ready to head home, Mr. Ralph Lauren came up to her and said, "Hello, beautiful. May I buy you a drink?"

"Oh, no, I'm afraid I'm only drinking water tonight," Liv blurted out.

"Well, then, may I please buy you a water?"

Liv could feel herself begin to blush. "Sure."

Mr. Ralph Lauren ordered Liv another sparkling water, and a tequila and tonic for himself.

"So, gorgeous, do you always only drink water, or is this some kind of special occasion?"

"Actually, tonight is sort of a special occasion," replied Liv.

"Well now I'm intrigued, beautiful. What's so special about tonight?"

"I'm getting divorced."

"Hot damn," he said as he slapped the bar with his hand. "This must be my lucky day. So, please allow me to introduce myself. I'm James Foster, but you can just call me Mr. Right." He extended his hand to shake Liv's.

He's got to be kidding, Liv thought and then said, "It's very nice to meet you, James. I'm Liv Donovan."

"Liv, as in short for Olivia?"

"Yes, I was named after my grandmother."

"I've always loved that name. So, tell me, Liv, what fool in their right mind would leave a beautiful, classy, sexy woman like yourself?"

Liv giggled. Over the next hour, she shared everything about herself with James—her marriage, her children, her illness, her charity, and her upcoming golf event.

"Well, Olivia, I must say you are one hell of a woman. And I have no doubt that you won't be single for long. That being said, I would love to take you to dinner sometime." He reached into his pocket and pulled out his phone. "What's your phone number, beautiful?" Liv recited her phone number for the second time that evening.

"So, handsome, I have a question for you," she said.

"Okay, shoot."

"Well how come a gorgeous guy like yourself is single?"

James took a big sip of his cocktail and then placed his glass down on the bar. "Well, Liv, I actually just got out of a two-year relationship.

She kept pressuring me to get married, but I just knew she wasn't the one. Do you know what I mean?"

"Believe me, I completely understand," Liv replied. "So one last question."

"Go ahead."

"How old are you, exactly?"

"I just turned thirty-two."

"Well, James, I do have a small confession to make to you. I'm a little older than you are."

"How much older, beautiful?"

"Guess."

"Thirty-seven, thirty-eight tops."

Liv smiled and quickly answered, "You guessed it. I'm thirty-eight." Liv decided there was no need at this point to tell James that she was really forty-three.

"Olivia, I'm sorry to say this, but I really must be heading out. I have an early tee time tomorrow morning, but I promise to shoot you a text later. Oh, and by the way, I know my law firm would be more than happy to play in your golf event."

"Really?"

"Sure. It sounds like a terrific organization. I'll tell you what, we can discuss it over dinner next week." Then he kissed Liv's hand. "So glad we met."

"Me too," Liv replied. She smiled as James walked away.

Austin came up to her and said, "Well, Mom, it looks like you're having a good time. So who is he?"

"His name is James Foster. He's thirty-two and he's an attorney. Oh, and by the way, he thinks your mother's thirty-eight."

In a teasing voice, Austin asked, "Did you give him your phone number?"

"Yes, as a matter of fact, I did."

"See, I told you that you'd have fun tonight."

"Well, you were right. Tonight has been a lot of fun, but I think I should be heading home now."

Just then, William interrupted. "Mom, a bunch of us want to head on over to Cucina's with Beau and his brothers. Do you want to come?"

"William, I was just telling Austin, I really should be heading home. It's way past my bedtime."

Then Beau cut in to say, "I'm sorry, William. No Cucina's for me tonight. I have to get up early to go fishing with my dad tomorrow. But don't worry, my brothers still want to go."

"Okay, another time then. Hey, could you do me a favor, Beau? On your way back down to Delray, could you drop off my mom?"

"Sure," said Beau. "No problem."

"Wait," said Liv, "are you sure?"

"Of course. It's on the way."

Liv said goodnight to her sons and thanked them for such a fun evening. Out front, the valet pulled up Beau's Toyota Tacoma with the largest oversized tires that Liv had ever seen. Beau helped Liv climb up into the passenger seat.

"Wow," said Liv, "this is like being in a cockpit."

"Do you like it?" asked Beau.

"I love it."

Beau turned on some country music as they cruised through town. "Liv, I couldn't help noticing that you spent most of the night talking to that pretty boy. Let me just give you some friendly advice. I'd be careful of his kind, if you know what I mean. But on the other hand, with me, it's what you see is what you get."

"Well, Beau, I will definitely keep that in mind," said Liv.

Beau pulled into Liv's driveway, jumped out, and quickly ran around to open her door. He extended his hand to help her out of his truck. *How thoughtful.* Kurt hadn't opened a door for her in years. "Come on, I'll walk you to the door."

As they stood on Liv's front porch, Liv said, "Beau, thanks so much for driving me home."

"It was my pleasure. So would you like to come down to my family's bar sometime? My brothers have a band and they play every Thursday night."

"Can the boys come?"

"Of course."

"Great. I'd love to come down some time."

"So what's your phone number?"

Beau pulled out his phone, and for the third time that evening, Liv recited her number. Beau put Liv's number into his phone and then turned it around. At the top of the screen it read: "Love."

"Oh, Beau, you made a mistake. My name is Liv."

"No mistake. I think you're lovely." He leaned over and gave her a quick kiss on the cheek. As he walked down the driveway, he called out, "Just remember what I told you about those pretty boys." Liv laughed and shook her head as Beau jumped up into his truck and peeled out of her driveway.

Liv unlocked her front door and then went upstairs to get ready for bed. As she pulled her sheets back and was about to climb into bed, she received a text message: *Can't wait to take you to dinner. James XX.*

Wow, what a night this has been, she thought. *Maybe this whole being single thing won't be so bad after all.*

She texted back: *Sweet dreams, handsome. Looking forward to it. Liv XO.* As she hit the send button, Liv knew at that moment the next chapter of her life was about to begin.

CHAPTER 3

Liv's New and Exciting Possibilities

To kick off Liv's first golf event, she decided to host a dinner party at her home the night before. The theme of the evening was a country-style dinner complete with fried chicken, pulled pork, corn on the cob, baked beans, coleslaw, potato salad, and macaroni salad. The caterers had set up tables all around the pool deck that were decorated with red-and-white-checkered tablecloths, hurricane lanterns, and sunflower centerpieces. White string lights were hung across the backyard and country music filled the air.

For Liv, the last few weeks had been a whirlwind. Chase Montgomery was coming over once a week to cook dinner for the family. It turned out that he really was a whiz in the kitchen after all, and Rose loved being his little sous-chef. He also had been golfing with the boys over at The Breakers several times, and Austin was over the moon to have him back in town. To put it simply, Chase was a hard guy not to like. He was average in height and build, with jet-black hair, and stunning, blue-green kaleidoscope eyes. Chase also had a warm, loving smile, and a true gentleness about him. In short, he was the exact opposite of Kurt in every way. And over the last few weeks, Liv found herself looking forward to their weekly dinners. She was also extremely grateful for the kindness that Chase had shown toward her and her children.

Speaking of kindness, Beau Walker sure had surprised Liv. He started calling her every morning at 7:35 to say good morning and to see what her plans were for the day. From the first night that they met, Liv had felt very comfortable around Beau. She had even taken Beau up on his invitation to come down to his family's bar/restaurant, "The Shipwreck." The Shipwreck was a large, outdoor establishment located on the Intercoastal that Beau's family had owned and operated for over twenty years.

His brother's band, the Walker Brothers, was also quite the crowd-pleaser, playing everything from Jimmy Buffett and Kenny Chesney to Bruce Springsteen. To say that Beau and his brothers were wild was an understatement. To Liv, these brothers seemed to be untamable, with every woman in Delray chasing after them in the hopes of tying one of them down. But as far as Liv could see, that wasn't going to happen anytime soon. These brothers were having way too much fun. Beau was tall and thin with light brown hair and electric blue eyes that screamed mischief. After Liv learned of Beau's wild reputation, his commitment to her and her children was all the more surprising. He started coming to the house for dinner every Monday night, and he had even taken the boys out fishing a few times on his boat, *Seas the Day*.

Liv had also gone out on a couple of dinner dates with James Foster, and he had even agreed to be her date for the golf event. The first time James came to pick her up for their first date, Rose ran into his arms yelling, "Daddy! Daddy!" Liv had never been so embarrassed in her life, but James seemed to take it all in stride. He knelt down and picked her up right away. Then he said, "Before I take your mommy out to dinner, what do you say I read you a quick book?" Rose was thrilled.

She ran up to her bedroom and returned with the book *Green Eggs and Ham.* James gently picked Rose up and placed her on his lap while he read the book.

So, as you can see, Liv's house was now a bustle of activity and the mood of her home had dramatically changed since Kurt's departure. There seemed to be a happiness and peacefulness about it once again.

But Liv still did have one problem. In two days, The family was supposed to head up to Sea Island, Georgia, for their annual summer vacation. Liv had called the resort and begged to get out of their cottage rental agreement. "We're sorry, Mrs. Donovan, but as you know, you have to cancel within sixty days. We are now well past that timeframe, and at this point your deposit is non-refundable." The deposit was $18,000. That's right. Kurt had stuck her with an $18,000 vacation knowing he was leaving her.

Liv finally broke down and confessed her dilemma to William. "William, what are we going to do? I can't imagine walking into the same house that we have been staying in all these years without your father, but I can't get us out of the cottage rental agreement."

"Look, Mom, we're all just going to have to get used to him being gone, and I also think it's important that we carry on our family traditions."

"I don't know, William."

"Well, Mom, if it's all right with you, I can invite a few of my friends to come along. I also know Beau would love to join us, and Chase mentioned his grandparents have a house on the island and he was already planning on going up there for the Fourth. And I'm pretty sure that my friend Amanda would be happy to help you out with Rose. Mom, in my opinion, we need to make this the best Sea Island trip ever!"

"All right, son. So I guess, Sea Island, here we come!"

That evening, as Liv stood in her backyard with her children and a house full of people, she felt extremely proud. The golf event was sold out. Dr. Grubb was flying in from Toledo in the morning and Liv was beginning to feel that her life was full of new and exciting possibilities.

CHAPTER 4

The Golf Event

The next morning, Liv woke up bright and early, excited and nervous about hosting her first golf event. The event was taking place at The Breakers Golf Club, and the dinner/silent auction was being held in the Flagler Steakhouse. Liv, of course, had spared no expense on the fundraiser and had overseen every last detail, from the blue and white hydrangea centerpieces to the custom-made golf shirts and the over-the-top dinner menu.

The schedule for the day's event was as follows:

10:30: Golfers' registration

11:30: BBQ lunch on the veranda

1:00: Shotgun

5:00 to 6:30: Cocktails, silent auction, raw bar, and passed hors d'oeuvres

6:00: Buffet dinner, which included a salad bar, carving station, pasta station, and dessert bar.

Liv's goal was to give the golfers a day that they would never forget, and, hopefully, raise a considerable amount of money for POTS research.

At 10:30, Liv was over at The Breakers greeting golfers as they checked in for the day's events. She glanced across the room and noticed

David Santoro standing in the lobby. She ran over to thank him for all that he had done for her, personally and for the event.

"Anything for you, Liv. You know that." As she gave him a big hug, she spotted her children walking through the main entrance of the golf club.

"Look, David, my kids are here." She grabbed his hand and rushed over to them and said, "Don't you all look handsome in your golf shirts! You remember David Santoro, right, boys?"

"Sure," said William.

"Are you boys ready to have some fun out there today?" asked David.

"Can't wait. I've been looking forward to this for weeks," said Austin.

"And, Mom, these golf shirts and gift bags are awesome," said Jeffrey.

"He's right! Mom, this place looks great," added Austin.

"Your mother has done an amazing job and you should all be very proud of her," said David.

"Thanks, David," said Liv. "So, boys, after you're all done checking in, can you please do me a huge favor and help me greet the other guests?"

"Sure, Mom, no problem," said Jeffrey. "Whatever you need."

The professional photographer interrupted them to take some pictures of Liv, David, and her children. The next person Liv spotted across the room was Chase. She made her way over to greet him.

"Hi, Chase. Thanks so much for coming," she said as she gave him a hug.

"Of course, Liv. I'd like you to meet my dad's business partner, Bill Pittman, and this guy right here is my boss, Bob Morris."

"This is quite a turnout," said Arthur.

"Dad," said Chase, "Liv has been working tirelessly for months to pull this event together."

"I must say, it certainly has been a tremendous amount of work," said Liv, "but it looks like it's going to be a great day after all, and of course, I'm very pleased with the large turnout."

"Olivia, I wanted to thank you for having Chase over to your place so often for dinner," said Arthur. "He's really been enjoying himself over there. And he also seems to be quite taken with Rose."

Just then, Rose ran across the room straight into Chase's arms.

"Well, as you can see, the feeling is quite mutual," replied Liv, and they all laughed. Luckily, the photographer was right there to capture this touching moment. "Did you all get a chance to check in yet?" Liv asked.

"No, not yet," replied Chase.

"Well, please, head on over to the registration table to check in and get your golf shirts. Also, I'm pretty sure that they just started to serve lunch out on the veranda."

"Sounds great," said Chase as he put Rose down and gave Liv a hug. Then he whispered in her ear, "You've done a fantastic job."

"Thank you. I'll see you outside," she whispered back.

Liv stood back for a moment to take in the room when suddenly James Foster came up from behind her, hugged her, and kissed her on the cheek. "So, how is the woman of the hour doing?"

"Nervous, but it all seems to be going well so far."

"Well, I have no doubt that this will soon become the most popular golf event on the island," said James. "Hosted by the most beautiful woman on the island."

"Stop that, James," said Liv.

"Liv, I'm being serious. Just look at this place, and it's your first event. You should be very proud."

"Thanks, James. Now, listen, why don't you go ahead and check in? Dr. Grubb just arrived and I want to go say hi."

"Okay. You go do your thing and I'll see you later."

Liv walked over to greet Dr. Grubb.

"Hi, Blair!" she said, giving him a hug. "I'm so glad you're here."

"Olivia, I wouldn't have missed this for the world," said Dr. Grubb. "Now, let me introduce you to everyone. This is Harry Norman, the head of fundraising for the hospital; cardiologist, Mark O'Hare; and, last but not least, emergency room doc, Chris Jackson."

"Thank you all for coming," said Liv.

"We're all very excited to be here," said Harry Norman.

"And, Olivia, just so you know," Chris said, "Blair and I are wizards in the operating room, but I don't think you're going to be very impressed by our golfing skills out there today."

They all laughed and Liv said, "Just go out there and have fun. Now, if you'll please excuse me, I need to make sure that everyone has checked in and then I'll catch up with you all outside."

Liv walked over to the registration table. "Is everyone here?"

Sally, her event planner, looked over the guest list. "Everyone seems to be here except for Beau Walker."

"What? Are his brothers here? Ty, Tanner, and Dalton?"

"Oh, yes, they checked in about forty-five minutes ago and, man, are they gorgeous."

Where could Beau be? Liv thought. She pulled out her cell phone and texted him: *Beau, where are you?*

No reply.

"Don't worry," said Sally. "I'm sure he's on his way. Meanwhile, we need you downstairs so we can take the group photo."

"Okay," said Liv.

When Liv got downstairs, she ran up to Austin. "Austin, where's Beau?"

"Wait, he's not here?"

23

"Nope."

"Mom, Don't worry. There's no way he would miss this. Trust me."

"Well, Austin, where can he be? We're supposed to start in five minutes."

"Mom, I guarantee you he'll be here."

The announcement was made for all of the golfers to get into their assigned golf carts and just then, Liv heard, "Love, Love, I'm here!" Beau was running across the practice green tucking in his golf shirt and finishing putting on his belt. He ran up and embraced her.

"Beau, where have you been?"

"I'm sorry I'm late, Love. But you didn't think I'd miss this, did you?" He kissed her on the cheek and Liv giggled.

"You're something else, Beau Walker."

Liv went up and took the microphone, thanking everyone for coming. "I hope you all have a great time out there. And just remember, the beverage and cigar cart will be riding around on the course all day. Fireball shots are being served at hole number seven. And last but not least, don't forget to give the hot shot cannon a try. Whoever gets a hole in one wins a weekend getaway to Vegas. Good luck, gentlemen, and I'll see you out on the course!"

The golfers lined up and they were off.

As Liv watched them go, the golf pro for The Breakers walked over.

"Hi, I'm Brodie Anderson," he said. "Sally thought it would be nice if I drove you around the course for a bit."

"Sure."

They got into the golf cart and soon began making small talk.

" I can't help but notice your accent," said Liv. "Where are you from originally?"

"Scotland. But I've been in the States for almost fifteen years now."

As they drove around, Liv loved seeing everyone out on the course, and all of the golfers seemed to be having a great time.

"So, I heard you're getting divorced," said Brodie.

Oh, Lord, thought Liv. *The whole world knows.* "Oh, yes," she said.

"Are you seeing anyone?"

"Well, I've been out to dinner a few times with…oh, there he is. The guy with the seersucker shorts."

"Is it serious?"

"To tell you the truth, I'm not really sure. I'm still pretty new at this."

"So, I'd like to give you my phone number if that's okay."

What? Liv thought. "Um, sure, I guess that would be okay."

"Maybe we could go out to dinner sometime? And by the way, this really is a very impressive event."

"Thank you," replied Liv.

Soon, they returned to the clubhouse and Liv thanked Brodie for the ride. Then she went home to take a shower and change into her white cocktail dress.

At 5:00, she was back at The Breakers in the Flagler Steakhouse, making sure everything was in place for the rest of the evening. The room looked beautiful and Liv finally felt as though all of her hard work had paid off.

The golfers were downstairs in the locker room, changing and slowly making their way upstairs for the cocktail hour and silent auction. David came up the stairs first.

"Did you have fun?" Liv asked.

"Liv, it was so fun. You did a great job. Everyone was having a ball out there."

Liv couldn't help but notice how handsome David looked in his pink polo. "Would you like to buy me a drink?"

"Of course, but I thought it was an open bar."

"It is." They both laughed. They walked across the room to the bar and David handed Liv a glass of champagne.

"Cheers to us."

Liv took a sip. "David, I can't believe you never got married," she said.

"I gave my heart away years ago. You know that."

Liv smiled. "But you would make such a great husband and father."

David smiled in return. "We'll see. Maybe someday."

Just then, Chase interrupted. "What a great day!" he said. "We all had so much fun out there. Liv, I see they have oysters, and I know how much you like them. Do you want to check out the raw bar with me?"

"Actually, I think David loves oysters even more than I do. Have you two met?"

"Oh, yes, we did a couple of fireball shots together at hole seven."

"Great, well let's go eat some oysters."

David, Liv, and Chase went over to the raw bar and then found a high-top table.

"The food is amazing," said Chase.

"It should be," said David. "Liv hand-selected the entire menu."

"I know she did." Chase reached across the table and squeezed Liv's hand.

At that moment, her boys, Beau, and Beau's brothers all came up from downstairs.

"Mom, What a day!" said Austin. "Can we do this every week?"

"Love," said Beau, "you killed it. I haven't had this much fun in years."

"I'm so happy you all had such a great time," said Liv. "Now, please go and get some food. I'm sure you must be starving."

"Mom, the food looks fantastic," said Jeffrey. "You did all of this?"

"Yes, Jeffrey."

"Well, Mom, I'm very proud of you." Liv hugged her boys, and then she went to chat with the other guests.

At 6:30, everyone was seated for dinner. Liv made a short speech thanking everyone for coming. "I know not everyone here knows what postural orthostatic tachycardia syndrome is, so my family and I have put together a video to help give you an idea of what we've all been going through these last few years."

The video featured Dr. Grubb, Liv, Rose, and testimonials from each of her sons. The background music was Sara Evans's *A Little Bit Stronger*. By the end of the video, there wasn't a dry eye in the room.

James held Liv's hand and said, "I'm so proud to be sitting next to you tonight. You're one hell of a woman, Olivia." Liv kissed him on the cheek.

After dessert, Dr. Grubb made a short speech thanking Liv and her family, then it was time for the check presentation. Much to Liv's surprise, she had raised over $25,000 that day for the Dr. Blair Grubb Endowment Fund for POTS Research.

When almost all of the guests had left, Liv decided to invite a few people to come back to her house. They all gathered in the backyard, drank champagne, and listened to music. James and Liv were sitting on a bench together and Rose had fallen asleep on James's lap.

"What a day," James said. "Can I tell you something?"

"Of course."

"There is nowhere else in the world that I'd rather be right now than sitting here next to you with your daughter sleeping on my lap. Liv, this feels right, doesn't it? I mean look at us. We look like a family."

Liv looked down at Rose and at her boys across the yard. She did have to admit, she felt happy. But the question in Liv's mind was...*Is this love?*

CHAPTER 5

Cheers to Being Back on Sea Island

Two days after the golf event, Liv was traveling to Sea Island, Georgia, in a caravan of cars. She was riding with Beau and Rose, followed by William, Austin, Jeffrey, and Amanda. Behind them were three of the boys' friends—Greg, Jake, and Chad.

As the convoy headed north on I-95, Liv was filled with mixed emotions about returning to the island. She realized more than ever that she was now solely responsible for keeping all of their family traditions alive. And on top of that, she was struggling with her new role as a single mother.

Unfortunately, James Foster was unable to take time off from work to join Liv and the family, but, luckily, Chase would be driving up the following day to stay at his grandparents' home on the island. He had even arranged to take the following week off so he could be there for the entirety of Liv's vacation.

As they all drove over the Sidney Lanier Bridge, Liv got a huge pit in her stomach. When her boys were very young, she had made up a song about going to Sea Island to the tune of *It's the Most Wonderful*

Time of the Year. When her car reached the top of the bridge, her cell phone rang. Her three boys were all singing in unison:

> *"It's the most wonderful day of the year,*
> *We're heading to Sea Island and we're all full of good cheer,*
> *because it's the happiest, happiest day of the year."*

Liv's eyes filled with tears. "You boys are too funny." They drove up next to her, rolled down their windows, and were singing at the top of their lungs.

Beau reached over and grabbed her hand. She looked at him with tears in her eyes. "Beau, I will never understand how a man could walk out on those three fantastic boys. Not to mention the little princess who's sound asleep in the back seat."

"Love, he's not a man. Not in my book, anyway."

No, he's not, Liv thought. She had forgiven Kurt for walking out on her, but she would never forgive him for turning his back on his children.

"And, Love," Beau continued, "I wouldn't waste your time trying to figure him out. He's just not worth it. I think what you should do is focus on the kids and building a future with someone who truly deserves you." Then he kissed her hand.

"You're right," said Liv, as she squeezed his hand.

"And, Love, please stop worrying. This is going to be a great vacation. I promise."

"Well, between you and me, I sure could use one. These last few months have been exhausting."

Finally, after driving for nearly five hours, all three cars pulled into the cottage rental office parking lot.

"I'll go inside and get the house keys and the membership cards," said Liv.

"Take your time," said Beau. "I'll look after the troops."

As soon as Liv entered the cottage rental office, the receptionist behind the desk said, "Welcome back, Mrs. Donovan."

"Thank you. It's so nice to be back."

"Here is your welcome-back cottage rental packet. And if you could just sign right here, I have the keys for your usual cottage—Beach Club Garden North, suite 434. And inside the packet are the parking passes for your vehicles and your membership cards. I must say, Mrs. Donovan, you have quite a large group with you this year."

"That I do," replied Liv, nodding. "Thanks again for your help."

Liv returned to the car and all three cars filed out of the parking lot. As they drove down Sea Island Road with the marshes on each side of the car, the marsh bunnies were making their on-time evening appearance. Liv rolled down her window and took in a deep breath of that wonderful briny air that she had come to love so much over the years.

When they pulled up to the guard gate, the security guard said, "Welcome back, Mrs. Donovan."

"Thank you. It's great to be back." Then she whispered to Beau, "I'm definitely going to have to change my name. *Mrs. Donovan* has got to go."

After the guard waved them all through, they found parking spots in front of the oceanfront cottage and began unloading the cars.

"I'll go on ahead and unlock the house," Liv said. But as she put the key in the door, she suddenly felt ill. The familiar smell of the cottage mixed with all of the memories from trips past came flooding back. She slowly walked into the master bedroom and found herself staring at the bed, recalling all of the years of sleeping next to Kurt under the wooden-beam ceiling. She sat down on the bed and began to cry.

Beau walked in. "Love, Are you okay?"

"Beau, I think that maybe this was a huge mistake."

He sat down next to her. "No, Love, it's definitely not. The boys are so excited to be here. They're picking out their bedrooms and unpacking. Now, listen, Love, you need to be strong for them. They deserve this vacation just as much as you do."

"I know, Beau. And you're right. But can you please do me a favor and take everyone down to the beach so I can have some time alone to pull myself together?"

"Of course." Walking out of the bedroom he called out, "Hey, everybody, we're all going down to the beach for a game of touch football before dinner."

After they all left, Liv unpacked her suitcase and put the groceries away. She then went into the living room and opened the large sliding glass door to allow the cottage to be filled with that intoxicating Georgia sea air.

Just as she stepped out onto the balcony, her cell phone rang. It was James.

"Hey, beautiful. How's it going up there?"

"It's good," said Liv. "The drive was easy. I'm just getting the house in order and everyone else is down on the beach."

"Do you miss me?"

"Of course I do."

"So where's Beau?"

"He's down on the beach. Why do you ask?"

"Olivia, I'd be careful with him if I were you."

"James, what are you trying to say?"

"Liv, he has quite the reputation with the ladies, as you know."

"James Foster, are you jealous of him?"

"No, never. Not in a million years. I'm just saying don't let your guard down around him."

31

"All right, handsome. I can assure you there's no need to worry. But, listen, I really need to go and set the table for dinner. We're staying in tonight and ordering room service."

"Okay. I'm glad you made it up there safe and sound, and I'll text you later."

"Thanks, James." She hung up the phone and went to work setting the dinner table for ten. She found a white tablecloth, placemats, and napkins in the walk-in pantry. She grabbed a pair of scissors from the kitchen and went down by the pool to cut some pink and blue hydrangea for the centerpiece. Next, she placed the dinner plates and silverware on the table. She stepped back to admire her work. At six, she picked up the phone and called room service. "Yes, I'd like to place a dinner order for ten, please, and I'm going to try to make this as simple as possible. We're going to have nine orders of shrimp cocktail, nine Caesar salads, and nine filet dinners. All medium rare, please. And one kid's chicken tender dinner with fries, delivered to Beach Club Garden North, 434."

"Okay, Mrs. Donovan, we'll have everything over to you within the hour."

"Great. And thanks so much."

Liv jumped into the shower and then changed into a casual summer dress. When she walked out into the living room, Beau was sitting on the couch looking through a coffee table book about the island.

"Well, don't you look lovely?" he said. "And the table looks beautiful."

"Thanks, Beau. So where is everyone?"

"Showering and getting ready for dinner. By the way, Amanda is great with Rose."

Just then, the doorbell rang. "That must be dinner," said Liv.

"Okay, I'll go tell everyone that it's here."

Liv opened the door and two men from room service came in, lit votive candles, and set out the dinners. Liv thanked them and signed the bill.

"We're so glad you're back on the island, Mrs. Donovan. Just give us a call when you're finished and we'll come back to remove everything."

"Thank you. It all looks perfect."

Liv closed the door behind them and then put on the song *Georgia on My Mind*. Once everyone was gathered around the dinner table, Liv raised her wine glass and made a toast. "Cheers to being back on Sea Island."

They all clinked glasses and then Beau raised his glass and said, "Cheers to you, Love, for arranging this fabulous vacation and perfect first dinner."

"Yes, thanks, Mom, this is awesome," said Austin.

"It really is," agreed William.

"We're eating like kings tonight," said Jeffrey. "Mom, after dinner we all really want to go to bingo, if that's okay."

"Beau, do you want to come with us?" asked William.

"No," said Beau, "I think I'll stay in with your mom and Rose tonight."

"That sounds fine, William," said Liv, "but please remember the bingo dress code: jackets and ties. And Amanda, did you bring a cocktail dress?"

"Oh, yes," replied Amanda. "Don't worry, William told me all about bingo."

"Mrs. Donovan," asked Chad, "why do we have to get all dressed up to go to play bingo?"

"Because, Chad, you're staying at a place that's rich in Southern tradition," answered Liv. "But don't worry, I promise it will all make sense once you get there."

After dinner, the boys and Amanda went to their rooms to change for bingo. Room service returned to remove the dinner plates and left a welcome-back dessert tray—pecan pie, warm chocolate chip cookies, and strawberry tarts.

"Wow," said Beau when he saw the dessert tray. "They sure know how to spoil you here."

"That they do," said Liv.

The kids all came out into the living room dressed in their evening bingo attire.

"Let me go grab my camera," said Liv. "I want to take a few pictures before you leave." The kids lined up in front of the fireplace as Liv captured the moment. "I think I got a few good ones. Now, go and have fun. But please, remember your manners."

After the kids left, Liv tucked Rose in for the night. She returned to the living room and asked Beau, "Would you like to sit out on the balcony for a bit?"

"That sounds perfect," said Beau. "I think I'll have a bourbon and cigar, if that's okay."

"Of course."

Liv and Beau sat out on the balcony. "This really is one of the most peaceful places on earth," said Liv.

"I couldn't agree more. And would you just look at all of those stars," said Beau. "Our night sky back home looks nothing like this."

"Beau, I've been coming here my entire life and I'm telling you it never gets old."

"So when did Kurt first come here with you?"

"I guess the first time we came here was when William was around two, and then we just kept coming back every summer."

"Well, see, there you go, Love. This is *your* island, not his. You need to focus on making new memories here."

"You're right, Beau. And I'm so grateful you're here."

"Believe me, Love, there's no place that I'd rather be," said Beau. "So what do you say we make a wish on a star?"

Liv nodded, then closed her eyes and made a wish. Opening her eyes, she gazed up at the night sky, hoping that all of her wishes would come true.

CHAPTER 6

Shrimp and Grits

The following morning, Liv woke up to the smell of bacon and coffee. She put on her robe and walked out to the kitchen. On the dining room table was A stack of pancakes, a platter of scrambled eggs, and toasted bagels with cream cheese.

"Good morning, Love," said Beau, frying up a skillet full of bacon. "How did you sleep?"

"Pretty well, thanks," replied Liv, taking in the sight of the breakfast buffet. "Wow, I can't believe you did all of this." Over the course of her marriage, Kurt had only made her breakfast once a year, on Mother's Day.

"Can I pour you a cup of coffee?" asked Beau.

"Yes, please," replied Liv. Beau handed her a cup of coffee just as Rose and Amanda came into the kitchen followed by the boys.

"Wow," said Jeffrey. "This is great!"

"Yes, Beau decided to cook breakfast for everyone," said Liv.

"Thanks, man," said, Austin. "This is quite the spread."

"Well, you see, I'm hoping to get myself invited back," said Beau.

"Beau, if you do this every morning, I want you to come along on all of our family vacations from now on!" exclaimed William. They all laughed.

With full plates of breakfast, the boys sat down in the living room and put on ESPN.

"I think I'll have my breakfast out on the balcony," said Liv.

"I'll join you," said Beau.

Liv sat at the table on the balcony enjoying her breakfast and the gorgeous ocean view. Beau sat beside her and said, "This sure isn't a bad way to start the day," said Beau.

"No, not at all. It's so beautiful here."

Just then Liv got a text message: *Olivia, who the hell is James Foster, Chase Montgomery, and Beau Walker? I would like to know why these men are texting my wife at all hours of the day and night! Kurt.*

"Oh my God," said Liv.

"What's wrong?"

"It's Kurt. Look." Liv handed Beau the phone.

"He has some nerve," said Beau. "Are you still on his cell phone plan?"

"Yes, we all are."

"Well, when we get back home, we need to get you a new phone, a new number, and your own cell phone plan. He's keeping tabs on you through your phone."

"He's unbelievable," said Liv. "He leaves me, and now he's mad that I'm dating. What did he expect?"

"Look, Love, let's not let him ruin this beautiful morning."

"I know. You're right."

William opened the sliding glass door and said, "Beau, We're all going over to rent bikes for the week and then take a ride around the island. Do you want to come?"

"You should go, Beau," said Liv. "And besides, I'm going to get changed and head off on my morning beach walk."

"Okay," said Beau. "But, William, let's clean up the kitchen first before we head out."

"Have fun, and thanks again for breakfast," said Liv.

Liv put on her workout clothes and then walked down to the beach. It was a glorious day on the island. Liv decided to call Abbey Goldstein, her attorney, to let her know about the text message.

"Olivia, this is no surprise," Abby told her, after hearing of the text. "They don't want you, but they don't want anyone else to have you either. Typical. Listen, don't worry about any of this. And please don't text him back. Just enjoy your vacation with the family. And when you return, I'll address this with his attorney."

Liv felt a little better after talking with Abby, but she was still furious. *Leave me and my children alone!* she thought.

Just then, Chase called to tell Liv he was on his way. "I should be there around four," he said.

"Great," said Liv. "I made a reservation tonight for all of us at 6:30 over at Halyard's. Best shrimp and grits on the island."

"That's for sure," said Chase. "I'll be thinking about those shrimp and grits all day. I'm going to meet you all over there if that's okay. I want to spend some time with my grandparents when I first get there."

"Of course," said Liv. "Drive safe and I'll see you soon!"

Liv hung up and stared out at the ocean. She noticed a large school of dolphins playing in the surf. She smiled and took in a deep breath of the warm sea air. She then decided nothing was going to ruin this vacation for her and her children.

The rest of the day included a picnic lunch on the beach, followed by swimming, sailing, touch football, and sandcastle building. The kids were having a ball. Beau opened the cooler and poured two glasses of champagne.

"Are you having fun?"

"I'm having a great time," said Liv.

"Cheers, Love!" They clinked glasses and drank their champagne. It was turning out to be the perfect day at the beach.

At 6:30, they all walked into Halyard's except for Rose and Amanda. Amanda had volunteered to stay home with Rose so Liv could enjoy a night out. Chase was at the bar waiting for them, enjoying a bourbon and ginger.

Austin went right over to greet him. "Bro, glad you made it!"

"It's great to be here," Chase smiled.

"So we're on for golf tomorrow with your grandfather?"

"You bet."

Liv walked up to Chase and gave him a hug. "Great to see you, handsome," she said.

"You too," Chase said.

Beau interrupted to tell them that their table was ready. Then the host showed them to their usual round table in the window. Once seated, Liv had Chase on her left and Beau on her right.

"Love, everything on the menu looks great," said Beau. "What do you recommend?"

"Oh, no," said William. "Here we go."

"What?" said Beau.

"My mom has this annoying habit of ordering for the table."

"That's not fair, William," said Liv.

William rolled his eyes. "Beau, you'll see. Just watch."

Just then, the waiter came over to the table. "Can I start you off with some cocktails and appetizers this evening?"

"Sure," said Liv. "We'll have three bottles of Rombauer Chardonnay and three bottles of the Stag's Leap cab. We'll also have three orders of the Buffalo calamari, three orders of the pot stickers, and three orders of the shrimp tacos to start, please."

"See? What did I tell you?" said William. They all laughed.

Over dinner, they shared stories of past vacations on the island as they enjoyed shrimp and grits, seared diver sea scallops, and fried green tomatoes.

"So what's on the agenda for tomorrow?" asked Beau.

"Well, Chase and I have a round of golf scheduled with his grandfather," Austin replied.

"I really want to go skeet shooting tomorrow," said Jeffrey. "Does anyone else want to come?"

"I do," said William.

"I was hoping to go on another morning bike ride," said Beau.

"Mom, what are our plans for tomorrow night?" Austin asked.

"Well, I thought we'd stay in and get takeout from the Frederica House, if that's okay," said Liv.

"Sounds great," said William. "And Mom, tonight after dinner we'll take you back to the house first, but then we all really want to head over to Bubba Garcia's in Redfern Village to check out the ladies."

"Oh, brother," said Liv.

"Beau and Chase, you have to come with us," said Jeffrey.

"That's right! No excuses, gentlemen," said William.

"Yes, you should both go," said Liv.

"I wish I could," said Chase, "but I'm exhausted. It was a long drive up here and we have an early tee time tomorrow."

"William, I'll come for one margarita," said Austin, "but I can't be hungover out on the course tomorrow."

"Beau, you should go," said Liv. "It will give you a chance to see more of the island."

"Okay, I'm in," said Beau.

"And you all don't have to take your mom home. I can drop her off. It's on the way," said Chase.

After paying the check, they all went their separate ways. Liv climbed into Chase's night blue Porsche 911 convertible and, as they drove slowly down Sea Island Drive, the crescent moon's reflection danced off the glimmering water of the marsh.

"What a beautiful night," said Liv.

"It sure is," said Chase, as he pulled into the cottage parking lot. "Come on, I'll walk you to the door. And, Liv, thanks again for inviting me to dinner."

"Are you kidding me? I'm so glad you came. Do you want to come over tomorrow night for dinner?" Liv asked as she put the key in to open the cottage door.

"I'll come on one condition."

"What is it?"

"On Wednesday night, you'll let me take you to dinner over at the Georgian Room."

"Wow, that's fancy, handsome."

"What do you say?"

"I say you have yourself a dinner date on Wednesday night."

Chase leaned over and kissed her on the cheek. "Sleep well, Liv."

"You, too."

Liv went inside and walked out onto her balcony. The waves were pounding on the shore and the palm trees were swaying in the warm night air. She looked up at the evening sky and saw Venus. *Make a wish*, she thought. She closed her eyes. *I wish for peace, love, and happiness.*

Just then she got a text: *Babe, are you still up? I haven't heard from you all day. James. XX.*

She turned off her phone. Somehow, she couldn't see a happy-ever-after in her future with James Foster. But if not with James, with who?

CHAPTER 7

The Spa

The next morning, Liv woke up to the same scene as the day before—Beau in the kitchen, whipping up a breakfast feast and the boys in the living room watching ESPN and recapping the events from the night before.

"Hey, Mom, I called over to the shooting center and I made us all a reservation for four o'clock today. Is that okay?" asked Jeffrey.

"Sounds great," replied Liv.

"I'll text Chase and Austin to see if they want to join us after they're done golfing," said Jeffrey.

"Beau, do you want to go for a morning bike ride again after breakfast?" asked William.

"Of course," Beau replied. "Love, are you going out on your morning walk?"

"Yes, I can't wait," Liv replied, and then turning toward Amanda, she said, "Amanda, is Rose still sleeping?"

"Like a rock," replied Amanda.

"All this salt air has really worn her out," said Liv. "Okay, I'm going to go get changed and then head down to the beach."

As Liv was out walking on the sandbar, she reached down and

picked up two sand dollars as the warm Georgia sea rolled in slowly over her toes. She had to admit to herself that she was surprised by how well the trip was going so far. *This island really does possess magical powers*, she thought.

When she arrived back at the cottage, she jumped into the shower and started to get ready for another day down on the beach. As she was finishing packing up her beach bag, the cottage house phone rang.

"Good morning, this is the Sea Island Spa calling. Is this Mrs. Donovan?"

"Yes?"

"Mrs. Donovan, we're calling to confirm your four o'clock couples massage for today. We've been trying to reach you on your cell phone all morning, but it's been going straight to voicemail."

"Oh, yes, I'm afraid I turned it off last night. And, also, to be completely honest, I forgot all about the spa appointment. You see, we've already made plans to go over to the shooting center this afternoon."

"Well, Mrs. Donovan, you booked this appointment way back in April. And, as you know, our cancellation policy is six hours in advance or we have to charge you."

"What would be the cancellation penalty?"

"$950, plus tax, and a twenty percent gratuity, I'm afraid."

Liv bit her lip. "Okay, no worries. We'll be there."

Damn, she thought as she hung up the phone. *What do I do now?* She didn't want to air out her dirty laundry to the spa staff and explain that her husband had recently left her. Liv walked out into the living room.

"What's wrong, Mom?" asked William. "You look upset."

"I am upset. A few months ago, I booked massages for your father and me, and, of course, I completely forgot. The spa just called to confirm our four o'clock appointments for today and if I don't go, they're going to charge me."

"How much?"

"Don't ask. It's a lot."

"Well, I'd go with you, but we're all super excited about skeet shooting."

"I'll go with you," said Beau casually, as he flipped through the morning paper.

"You will?"

"Sure, why not? Doesn't everybody like a good massage?"

"What about skeet shooting?"

"No big deal. I'll just go another time."

"Okay, Beau, and thanks. Well, let's all go down to the beach for a little while before we have to head over to the spa."

At 3:00, Beau pulled the car into the spa's parking lot. Next, they crossed over an arched footbridge that overlooked a koi pond. On the other side of the bridge was a massive, three-tier fountain that fed into a stream that ran from the koi pond to an indoor relaxation area.

Beau opened the spa door for Liv and said, "Wow, Love, would you look at this place?"

"I know. It's gorgeous, isn't it? Why don't you have a look around and I'll check us in," said Liv.

Beau went off to check out the spa and Liv walked up to the receptionist desk to check in.

"Hi," Liv whispered. "We're checking in. Mr. and Mrs. Donovan. Also, I was hoping you could do me a huge favor. You see, my husband always talks all throughout the massage. And I was wondering if there was any way you could put us into two separate treatment rooms?"

"Say no more, Mrs. Donovan," said the receptionist. "I completely understand, and I'll see what I can do."

When Beau reappeared, the receptionist said, "Okay, Mr. and Mrs. Donovan, if you will please follow Pam and Eric, they will show you to the locker rooms, and then, after you've changed into your robes, you can meet each other back at the indoor pond."

Liv went into the ladies locker room and changed into her white robe and slippers. She felt confident that she had taken care of what would have been an extremely awkward situation. She then met Beau back at the indoor relaxation area, where they sat together at the edge of the pond in two oversized chairs complete with a large ottoman.

The spa attendant brought over two glasses of champagne. Liv and Beau clinked glasses as the water from the pond trickled over the stones creating the sound of a waterfall.

"I feel like I'm in paradise," Beau said.

"It's something else, isn't it?"

Soon, two therapists appeared, a male and female. "If you would please follow us, Mr. and Mrs. Donovan," said the female therapist. Beau smiled and winked at Liv. Then they all entered the elevator and went up to the second floor. As they walked down a long corridor, there were single doors on either side and a huge set of double doors at the end of the hallway. Liv's heart was pounding as they passed each single door and kept walking towards the end of the corridor. At the end of the hallway, they all stopped suddenly as the male therapist pushed open the double doors. "Here we are," he said. "Welcome to our couple's suite."

Oh, God, Liv thought as she looked around the room. There was a fireplace, a claw-footed soaking tub with rose petals floating on top, a beautiful crystal chandelier, and a small living room area with a bottle of champagne on the coffee table. In the center of the room were two massage tables. The entire room screamed romance and sex. *What did I get myself into?* she thought.

"We're going to step outside for a moment," said the female therapist. "If you would please remove your robes and then lie on the tables face down. We'll knock before we come back in."

"Sounds perfect," said Beau with a huge grin on his face. And with that, the two therapists left the room.

"Beau, what are you smiling about? I asked for two separate rooms. This is a big mistake. I'm going to go and say something."

"Love, no you're not. Trust me. Everything is fine."

"Are you sure?"

"Yes, I'm very sure. I mean, would you just look at this place! And by the way, I really think you need this massage."

As Beau turned around to remove his robe, Liv quickly hung up hers and then dove under the sheet. There was a knock at the door. "Come in," said Beau. The two therapists entered.

"So, Mr. and Mrs. Donovan," said the female therapist. "I just looked over your information card and it says you've been married for twenty-one years. I must say, that's quite an accomplishment these days."

"It still feels like we're newlyweds to me," said Beau.

Oh, brother, thought Liv. For the next ninety minutes, Liv tried desperately to relax, but her mind and heart kept racing. Her therapist pulled the sheet down past her buttocks. *Can he see me?* she thought. *The only person who has seen me naked in the last twenty-one years is Kurt. Olivia Whittaker, how did you get yourself into this mess?*

Finally, the therapist said, "Okay, time's up. I hope you both enjoyed your massages and got a chance to relax. Please feel free to help yourself to the champagne. And as you know, you have the room all to yourselves for the next hour."

"Sounds great, and thank you," said Beau as the therapists left the room.

Liv was on her back. She turned her head and looked at Beau. "So, did you like it?"

"Love, this was hands down the best massage I've ever had. I think I even fell asleep for a while."

"You did. You were snoring."

"I was not!" They both laughed. Beau stood up and walked across the room naked to get his robe. Liv couldn't help but look. He did have a beautiful body.

She sat up and pulled the sheet up around her breasts. Nervously, she asked, "Beau, can you please bring me my robe?"

"Of course." He took the robe off the hook and walked up behind her. She reached up and put her right arm into the robe as he held it for her. She went to put her left arm in and as she did the sheet slipped down around her waist exposing her breasts. She looked up at him. He gazed deeply into her eyes and kissed her. It was the most passionate kiss of her life. He then began kissing her and touching her breasts. "I've been wanting to do this for a while now," he whispered.

"You have?"

"Yes." He walked over to the table and opened the champagne. He poured two glasses and handed one to Liv. "Cheers to us, Love." They clinked glasses and each took a sip. He leaned over and kissed her again. "What do you say we take advantage of the bathtub?"

Liv's heart was pounding. "Beau, I'm sorry, and please don't be disappointed, but I really think we should be getting back to the house," Liv nervously answered.

"Are you sure?" asked Beau.

"Yes, I'm sure. I'm so sorry, Beau, but I'm just not ready for all of this."

"That's okay, Love. You don't have to explain." They each took one more sip of champagne and kissed each other.

"Are you upset?" asked Liv.

"Love, I don't think I could ever be upset with you."

As they walked back down the corridor, Beau put his arm around Liv and then slipped his hand into hers. When they passed by the pond, they were still holding hands.

"Meet you back here?" Beau asked. She nodded. She turned to walk away, but he pulled her back toward him and kissed her one more time.

On the drive back to the cottage, Beau reached over and held her hand. He soon parked the car and then leaned over and kissed her. "Thanks for a lovely afternoon."

"You're welcome," she said. "And, Beau, thanks for understanding." Then she kissed him again.

When they walked into the house, the dinner table was set perfectly and the food was already on the table. "Wow, who did all this?" asked Liv.

"Amanda and Rose set the table," said William, "and Chase picked up the dinner."

"Well, it all looks amazing."

"So how was the spa?" asked Chase.

"Nice," replied Liv. She looked across the room at Beau. He smiled and winked at her.

Over dinner, they dined on some local favorites—fried oysters, broiled scallops, hogfish, okra, succotash, and fried mushrooms. "What a feast," said Beau.

"I'm stuffed," said Jeffrey.

"Well, why don't we clean up real fast before it gets dark and head down to Conch Island to walk off our dinner?" said Liv.

"Where's Conch Island?" asked Chase.

"Oh, my mom just calls it that," said William. "It's the beach just past the rock jetty. When we were little, we would always find a ton of conch shells down there."

"Gotcha," said Chase. "Well, I would really love to join you, but I should go and spend some time with my grandparents. They keep saying that they've hardly seen me since I've been here."

"Okay, but you are coming with us tomorrow night to Colt and Alison's, aren't you?" asked Jeffrey.

"Of course. I can't wait," said Chase.

"Oh, and, Chase, we have a ten o'clock tee time tomorrow morning over at The Lodge if you want to join us," said William.

"Okay, count me in. And, guys, thanks again for this afternoon." He turned to Beau and said, "Sorry you missed it, Beau."

"Next time," replied Beau.

"Oh, and just so there's no confusion, Beau, it'll just be me and Liv for dinner on Wednesday."

"What dinner?"

"Oh, I thought I told you," said Liv. "Chase is taking me over to the Georgian Room on Wednesday night."

"Interesting," said Beau.

"Come on, Chase," said Liv, "I'll walk you out." Liv walked Chase to the door. "Thanks again for picking up dinner. That was so very sweet of you."

"No problem. And, Liv, I'm really looking forward to dinner on Wednesday," replied Chase.

"Me too."

"Just making sure," Chase said, and then he kissed her on the cheek.

After Chase left, Liv turned toward everyone and said, "Okay, go grab your flipflops and let's go to Conch Island!"

As they walked over the rock jetty, the sunset made a fiery pink, orange, and red sky. All of the kids ran ahead with Rose trailing behind.

"Can I see your phone?" Beau asked.

"Sure," Liv replied. Beau began taking pictures of the brilliant sunset, the kids playing on the sandbar and Liv walking on the water's edge.

"Here," he said, handing her back the phone. "I want you to always remember this day."

"Beau Walker," she smiled, "I have come to realize I might not know much, but I do know I will remember this day forever."

And what a day it had been.

CHAPTER 8

The Fourth of July

Fourth of July morning, 2015. All of the guys had left bright and early for their day of golf over at The Lodge. Liv, Amanda, and Rose walked down to Sea Island Road to watch the annual Independence Day parade. Each house along the way was decorated with American flags and red, white, and blue pinwheels. The theme of this year's parade was "A Country Fair." Funnel cake stands, magic shows, and carnival games ran the length of the parade route. Rose was having a ball in her red, white, and blue Vineyard Vines swimsuit with matching hair bow that was the size of the state of Georgia. After Rose had played endless carnival games and was stuffed with funnel cake, cotton candy, and corn dogs, Liv decided it would be nice to spend the rest of the day on the beach. Liv and Amanda sat in two lounge chairs under an umbrella as Rose frolicked in the surf.

"She looks so happy, doesn't she?" asked Liv.

"I think Rose is the happiest little girl that I've ever met," replied Amanda.

"Well, I've been worrying about her," said Liv. "Every once in a while, she'll ask for her father. But since he traveled so much over the course of our marriage, I've been telling her Daddy's away for work. And if I'm being completely honest, I'm not just worried about her, but

51

about all of my children. I know this hasn't been easy on the boys, even though they've refused to discuss their father's sudden departure from their lives. And poor Austin. That kid finally thought he was getting the family of his dreams and then Kurt walks out. Anyways, Amanda, when you're a mom, you'll understand. What is that saying? 'A mother is only as happy as her unhappiest child.'"

"Sure, I get it," said Amanda. "And I guess you probably don't know this, but my dad left when I was two, so I can kind of understand what you've all been going through."

"Amanda, I must say, I'm very grateful that you came along on this trip with us. You've been so helpful with Rose and I can see why all three of my sons have been fighting over you for years."

Amanda laughed. "Mrs. Donovan."

"Amanda, Please call me Liv, remember?"

"Okay, Liv. Well, as you already know, you have the sweetest sons, but I think we have more of a brother-sister relationship at this point."

"Amanda, I know my boys and I think they're all quite smitten with you."

"Well, speaking of being smitten, I've been dying to ask you something."

"What is it? You can ask me anything."

"Which one do you like?"

"I'm sorry, I'm not sure I'm following you."

"Is it Beau or Chase?"

Liv laughed. "Well, to be honest, before we came on this trip, I was seeing someone back home. But since we've been here, I've kind of lost interest in him."

"Of course you did. You have Beau and Chase in hot pursuit of you at all times."

"Amanda, I think that maybe you've been out in the sun too long!"

They both laughed. "But seriously," said Amanda, "they're swarming around you like a couple of angry bees."

"Amanda, I really don't think that's true, and besides, I'm still trying to figure out this whole newly single situation that I've found myself in."

"So, would you like my advice?"

"Of course."

"Well, let's face it. Beau Walker is being chased by every girl in Delray and pretty much South Florida. And yes, he's beyond gorgeous. But as far as I know, he's never had a serious girlfriend, which to me is a huge red flag considering that he's in his thirties. Now, to be fair, I've only met Chase a handful of times over the years, but from what I've seen on this trip, it's clear to me that he truly adores you and Rose."

"Well, Amanda," Liv smiled, "I must say, I think you're wise beyond your years."

"All I'm saying is you might know your sons, but I know men and I can definitely see a storm brewing out on the horizon. I mean, did you see Beau's face when Chase told him that the two of you were going out to dinner? His blood was boiling. And, Liv, I'm telling you, being on this trip is better than any reality TV show."

Just then, Rose ran up and gave Liv a huge sandy hug. "Can we please go up to the pool now, Mom?"

"Sure," said Liv. "Saved by my child!"

"Nope, more like 'soon to be continued,'" They both laughed as they gathered up their things and headed to the pool.

Later that evening, they all piled into their cars and headed over to The Lodge for the Fourth of July dinner at Colt & Alison's Steakhouse, to be followed by Sea Island's spectacular Fourth of July fireworks display.

On the drive over to The Lodge, they passed under canopies of trees heavy with Spanish moss. And as soon as they turned down Retreat Avenue, Liv got goosebumps. Huge live oaks lined both sides of the road leading up to The Lodge. The Lodge's fountain lights had been changed for the evening and were now red, white, and blue. The Lodge itself looked like an English-style manor, dripping in Southern charm. Adirondack chairs were lined up like perfect soldiers on the manicured lawn that rolled down and kissed the Atlantic. Every night at sunset, the bagpiper would walk the lawn. As the bonfire was lit, children would gather to make s'mores while the grownups enjoyed their adult beverages in rocking chairs on the massive wraparound porch.

When Liv and the others stepped out of their cars, two valets greeted them and held open the huge double wooden doors that led into the lobby.

"Welcome back to The Lodge, Mrs. Donovan," said one of the valets.

"It's always nice to be back at my favorite spot," Liv replied.

Before heading off to dinner, they all gathered on the lawn at sunset for their annual Lodge family photos. Liv asked one of the waitresses if she wouldn't mind taking some group photos.

"I always have a photo from The Lodge on my Christmas card," she said.

"No problem," said the waitress. "You all look fantastic."

Liv had on a white cocktail dress. All of the guys were in seersucker suits except for William, who had decided to wear his navy blue pants embroidered with red lobsters, white shirt, and navy sports coat. Amanda was in a striking red cocktail dress, and Rose was twirling around on the lawn in her blue-and-white-striped dress embroidered with red sailboats. The Lodge's American flag waved gently in the background as the setting sun slowly dipped down into the Atlantic. The waitress took several group photos and then a few of just Liv and her children.

"Thanks so much," Liv said as the waitress handed her back the camera.

"No problem. I hope you all have a great night."

Next, they walked back inside to Colt and Alison's. The hostess escorted them to their usual window table that overlooked the eighteenth hole of the Plantation Golf Course. Liv loved how the mahogany-paneled walls, wood-burning fireplace, and exposed beams transported them all back in time to an elegant British dining hall.

The waiter appeared at the table and passed out the dinner menus. He then handed Liv the wine list, which was as thick as *War and Peace*.

"Wow, that's quite a list," said Chase. "May I have a look?"

"Of course," Liv said, handing him the book.

"Oh boy, you're in trouble now," said William.

"Why?" said Chase. "What did I do?"

All of Liv's sons burst into laughter. "Don't you remember the other night at Halyard's when she ordered for all of us?" said William.

"Chase, I'm pretty sure you just stole Mom's thunder," said Austin.

"You boys are too much," said Liv. "Chase, why don't we look through the wine list together?"

"Great idea," replied Chase.

"Oh, Lord. Now, we have two of them," said William. The entire table laughed. After looking closely through the wine list and dinner menu, Chase and Liv had made their selections. When the waiter returned to the table, Chase ordered three bottles of Faust and three bottles of the Ramsay Chardonnay. Liv ordered the appetizers, the seafood tower, steak tartare, and crab Maison.

"Mom, don't forget about the Caesar salad," said Jeffrey. Liv's boys loved how it was made tableside.

"Yes, and the Caesar salad for the table, please," Liv told the waiter.

"Mom, are we allowed to order our own dinners tonight?" asked William as he rolled his eyes.

"You're all on your own with the entrées," said Liv. "Except for Rose. My daughter will have the petite filet, medium, mashed potatoes, and broccoli." The waiter took the rest of the table's dinner orders as the sommelier poured the wine.

Liv raised her glass and said, "Happy Fourth. Cheers to family and friends." With that, they all clinked glasses.

Soon, the manager of the restaurant walked over to the table and said, "Welcome back, Mrs. Donovan. It's so great to see you and your children."

"Thank you. It's so nice to be back. And thank you for saving us our favorite table."

"Of course. Anything for you and your family. The staff and I always look forward to seeing the Donovan family. But wait—where is Mr. Donovan?"

Without a moment of hesitation, Jeffrey blurted out, "He died. Last fall in a car accident." The table fell completely silent.

"I'm so sorry to hear that," said the manager, looking shocked.

"Thank you," said William. "It's been a hard year for all of us, but we know that our father would want us to continue our family tradition by coming back to the island every summer."

"Of course. Well, once again, I'm so sorry for your loss. Please enjoy your dinner and this evening's fireworks."

The manager turned and left and as soon as he was out of earshot, Liv said, "Jeffrey, I can't believe you said that!"

"Why, Mom? Dad's gone. And let's face it, he's not coming back," he said as he buttered a biscuit and then took a bite.

"He's right, Mom," said William.

I guess they're right, Liv thought, but she still couldn't believe Jeffrey had said it.

Shortly, the waiter returned with the appetizers and all of the ingredients to make the Caesar salad. The rest of the evening was spent enjoying the fabulous wine, food, and great conversation. Liv looked around the table and was so grateful for each and every person sitting there. The dinner concluded with Bananas Foster, which was also made tableside. Rose's eyes grew wide as the waiter poured rum into the pan and then lit it on fire. The flames nearly touched the ceiling as Rose clapped with delight.

After dinner, they all settled into the Adirondack chairs on the lawn to watch the fireworks display. Just as the fireworks began, the waitress appeared with bourbon and cigars for the men, champagne for Liv and Amanda, and a Shirley Temple for Rose. The sky erupted into bursts of red, white, and blue as patriotic music filled the air. Liv looked up at the sky and realized at that moment, there was no need to wish upon a star. she had everything she had ever wished for on this glorious Fourth of July night.

CHAPTER 9

"May I Have This Dance?"

Wednesday night had finally arrived and, thankfully, Amanda had assisted Liv with picking out the perfect dress for her dinner with Chase. Amanda chose a pale pink cocktail dress to go with Liv's gold-sequined wedge heels.

"You look fantastic," said Amanda as Liv studied herself in the full-length mirror.

"Are you sure?" asked Liv. "I feel like a ball of cotton candy that you'd find on the Jersey boardwalk."

Amanda laughed. "I promise, it's perfect. And I know he's going to love it."

"Amanda, I just realized something. I don't have an evening bag."

"Let me go look in my room," said Amanda. "I'm sure I have something."

Liv looked at herself nervously in the mirror. Amanda returned with a small, pale pink purse that was covered with tiny roses.

"Look, it matches," she said.

"But this is Rose's purse. I can't take this to a five-star restaurant."

"Sure you can," said Amanda.

Just then, the doorbell rang. "Oh, boy, it must be him," said Liv. She looked at her phone. "He's fifteen minutes early. Is anyone else home?"

"No, just Rose. The guys haven't come back from clay shooting yet."

"Okay, good," said Liv.

"Yeah, it's a good thing Beau isn't here to see you leave on your date."

"Amanda, I wouldn't exactly call this a *date*."

"Well, let's look at the facts, shall we? Chase is taking you to dinner at one of the finest restaurants in the country. You're standing in front of me wearing a cocktail dress and it took you hours to do your hair and makeup. Liv, I hate to break this to you, but you're going out on a date with Chase Montgomery."

Liv reached up and grabbed her string of pearls. *Oh, God,* she thought. *Is this a date?*

"Look, Amanda," she said, "you have this all wrong. It's just a friendly dinner."

"Okay, whatever you say, but I believe your *friend* is ringing the doorbell."

"All right, I better go and let him in, but would you mind taking Rose over to the beach club for a swim and dinner?"

"Of course not."

"Thanks, Amanda."

"No problem. Now, just go and have fun on your friendly dinner."

Oh, brother, thought Liv as she rolled her eyes and walked towards the front door.

Liv's heart raced as she opened the door and saw Chase standing there. He was wearing a navy suit with a cobalt blue dress shirt and a matching blue-and-pink-striped tie. *Damn, he looks good,* she thought. *Maybe this really is a date after all.*

"Wow, you look beautiful," said Chase.

"Thank you, so do you." Liv could feel herself blushing.

"So I decided to drive over in my grandparents' golf cart," said Chase, "since we're just going across the street. I hope that's okay."

"Sure. I've never taken a golf cart to dinner before. But I guess there's a first time for everything."

They got on the golf cart and drove across the street to the main hotel at Sea Island, The Cloisters. The grand hotel was located on the banks of the Black River. The hotel was rich in history, full of elegance and Southern charm. The Cloisters was built in 1928 by Addison Mizner. Over the years, several US presidents, heads of state, and foreign dignitaries had stayed under its Spanish-tiled roof.

"Would you like to walk around the hotel for a bit before dinner?" asked Chase.

"I definitely would," replied Liv. "Let's go to the solarium first to see the lovebirds." Liv had always adored this room with its glass walls and greenhouse feel.

In the corner of the solarium were two beautifully hand-painted wooden cages that housed the peach and green lovebirds. Liv walked over to the cages.

"I'm back," she said. The birds slowly climbed down the cage toward her. "I come to see them every year, and I know this must sound silly, but I think they actually remember me," Liv said, turning to Chase. "My grandmother was obsessed with this room. So much so that she actually recreated it in her home in New Jersey, including the lovebirds. Let's go to the Spanish lounge next."

As they walked into the Spanish lounge with its stained-glass windows, massive wood-beamed ceiling, and stone fireplace, Liv could feel the history of the majestic hotel surrounding her.

"Liv, go stand next to the fireplace," said Chase, "so I can take your picture."

Liv posed in front of the fireplace, then said, "Chase, if we hurry, we can watch the sunset down on the dock."

Out on the dock, they watched as the sun slid slowly down behind the tall grass and cattails of the marshes. "Stunning, isn't it?" said Liv.

"Yes," replied Chase. "But I'm not talking about the sunset."

Liv could feel herself blush again. "Well, I guess we should be heading to dinner," she said nervously.

Chase offered his arm to escort Liv to the Georgian Room. As they walked past the three-tier fountain back into the enormous lobby, Liv asked, "How long have your grandparents had their house on Sea Island?"

"They actually built the house way back in the 1950s, so Sea Island has always felt like a second home to me. But, as you know, it has changed a lot over the years. Thankfully, the island's traditions still remain timeless."

"I couldn't agree more," said Liv.

"Speaking of Sea Island traditions, aren't the guys going to bingo tonight?"

"Of course," Liv replied. "My boys love bingo."

"Well, what's not to like? It's held in a beautiful ballroom with gorgeous women in attendance, two open bars, and a live band. Bingo is always a great evening."

"It certainly is," said Liv. She stopped as they strolled past the library. "Chase, would you just look at the woodwork in this room. The ceiling is carved to look as if it's covered with magnolia blossoms."

"Liv, I truly admire the way you appreciate the island's history just as much as I do."

They walked on and soon entered the Georgian Room.

"Good evening," said the hostess, "and welcome to the Georgian Room. Do you have a reservation with us this evening?"

"Yes," said Chase. "Party of two. Last name, Montgomery."

"Oh yes, we have you at a private table in the alcove as you have requested. If you'll please follow me, I'll show you to your table."

Liv smiled and held onto Chase's arm as they entered the beautiful dining room. The floor-to-ceiling windows allowed for the sunset to play off of the golden crystal chandelier. The dining room was opulent with its white columns, stone fireplace, and rich fabrics. A harpist played on a golden harp in the corner and Handel's harp concerto filled the air. The maître d' pulled out Liv's chair for her. He then took her purse and placed it on a pillowed stool beside her.

Five waiters attended to each table. It was said that the Georgian Room left an impression on you that would last a lifetime. So far, Liv was not disappointed. The maître d' handed Chase and Liv the dinner menus and placed the wine list on the table, a list even larger than the one from Colt & Alison's.

"Well, I guess we have some reading to do," joked Chase.

"Why don't we just have the same Chardonnay as the other night?" said Liv. "And, since this is such a special night, maybe the Caymus 40th Anniversary Cab."

"Perfect choices," said Chase. He waved over the waiter and ordered the wine. They both looked over their dinner menus. "Liv, would you like to do the chef's tasting menu?"

"Sure."

The waiter returned and opened the Chardonnay, and poured them each a glass. "Have we decided on dinner?"

"We're going to do the chef's tasting menu," replied Chase.

"Excellent choice," said the waiter. "Your first course will be the Maine lobster custard followed by frisée crispy egg, then the diver scallops with black truffles. Your fourth course will be the beef tenderloin with herb butter and locally grown vegetables."

"Wow, that seems like an awful lot," said Liv.

"Not to worry, miss," said the waiter. "Each plate is small and is truly a magnificent work of art. And I give you my word that you will not be disappointed."

"Okay, I think we're sold," said Chase. Chase raised his wine glass. "To many more beautiful dinners together." They touched glasses and each took a sip.

"Well, Chase, I don't know where we go from here," said Liv as she looked around the room. "You've set the bar very high tonight."

"Liv, I just thought with everything that you've been going through lately, that you deserved a special night out."

"Well thank you, Chase, and I want you to know that I really do appreciate all of this."

Over dinner, they talked about everything—their childhoods, families, first loves, colleges. The conversation never lagged and Liv felt completely at ease with Chase. Meanwhile, the dinner was spectacular. Each dish was masterfully plated with over fifty ingredients that must have taken hours and even days to prepare.

After the last course, Chase excused himself to use the restroom. As he returned, walking across the dining room, Liv noticed the way he carried himself. He moved with a sense of grace and confidence that Liv found to be very attractive.

Soon, the waiter reappeared and asked, "Have you decided on dessert? Now, if you want to try something truly exceptional, may I suggest our cheese trolley? It would pair beautifully with the wine you've selected this evening."

"What do you think, Liv?" asked Chase.

"I think it sounds delicious."

The waiter wheeled the cheese trolley over to the table and then placed four small pieces of locally made cheese on each of their plates with a fig preserve, Sapelo Farm honey, and nuts.

"Chase, I must say, this is hands down the best meal of my life," said Liv. Just then, her phone buzzed with a text message: *Love, are you coming to bingo? Beau.*

"Is everything okay?" asked Chase.

"Oh, yes. Beau just wanted to know if we're coming to bingo."

Chase took a sip of his wine. "Liv, whatever you want. We can go to bingo or get an after-dinner drink at the Georgian Room bar. I'm easy. I'll do whatever."

Liv had to admit that she was having a great time with Chase and she wasn't ready for it to end. She texted back: *I'm sorry Beau, but we're still at dinner. Have fun.* Then she glanced up at Chase. "Let's go to the bar."

"Sounds good to me," Chase replied, as he stood up and pulled out her chair.

They walked into the dark, candlelit Georgian Room lounge with its mahogany walls, wood-burning fireplace, and cozy, intimate, plum-colored velvet couches. A guitarist sat by the bar singing and playing Nat King Cole's song, "The Very Thought of You." The waitress came over to the table and asked for their drink orders.

"I'll have a glass of the Veuve Clicquot, please," said Liv.

"And I'll have a Woodford Reserve bourbon on the rocks with a splash of ginger," replied Chase.

The waitress soon returned with their drinks and Chase put his arm around Liv, pulling her next to him. "Cheers to a beautiful evening," he said.

As they each took sips of their drinks, Chase put his hand on Liv's thigh. Liv stared deeply into Chase's eyes and felt as though she could stay in this moment forever. The guitarist began to play "Stand By Me."

"May I please have this dance?" asked Chase. Liv nodded. They both slid off the couch. Chase took Liv in his arms and pulled her close.

He quietly sang to her as they danced. "Let me be him," he whispered into her ear. Liv looked up at him and thought, *What in the world is happening?*

When the song ended, they sat back down and finished their drinks. "I guess I should probably take you home now," Chase said.

"It is getting late," she answered quietly, but she really didn't want to go anywhere. They walked out front and a valet soon brought around the golf cart.

"Look at the moon," Liv said.

"It's full tonight," replied Chase.

Before long, they were back at the cottage.

"Chase, let's go up to the beach and look at the moon," said Liv.

"Sure."

They slowly walked down the lawn that led to the beach. The tall dune grass waved in the evening breeze as the moon reflected off of the Georgia sea.

"It's gorgeous," Liv said.

"Yes, it is," said Chase. Then he leaned down and kissed her. She felt her stomach do a somersault, something she had never experienced before. It was the perfect kiss at the perfect moment.

Liv bit her lip and asked, "Would you like to come in?"

"Are you sure?"

Olivia Whittaker, what are you doing? she thought, but then she kissed him again and all of her logic went right out the window. "Yes, I'm sure," she smiled.

When they entered the cottage, the house was quiet. The guys were all still at bingo and Rose and Amanda were both fast asleep. Chase kissed Liv one more time and then carried her into the bedroom. He unzipped her dress and she removed her panties, standing in front of him completely naked. He started kissing her neck. He slid his finger deep inside of her.

He loved how wet she was. She took off his tie and then ripped off his jacket. She helped him unbutton his dress shirt. She unzipped his pants, then slid her hand inside of his boxers and touched him. He wanted her. He kicked off his loafers, removed his pants, and laid Liv down on the bed.

He kissed her breasts and said, "I want to taste you." Then he moved slowly down her body and slid his tongue inside of her. Liv loved every second of it. He started kissing her neck again and slowly slid inside of her. "You feel amazing," he said.

She started moaning. "Chase, don't stop…please don't stop."

"I won't, I promise. I want you to cum."

"I'm going to cum now," she said.

"Me, too."

They both climaxed at the same time. Chase rolled over and placed his head on Liv's breast. She stroked his head and rubbed his back. Then he rolled over on his back and Liv put her head on his chest. She could hear his heart racing. He made small circles with his fingers up and down her arm.

"Are you okay?" he asked.

"I'm fine."

"Are you sure?"

"Yes. I thought I was going to be nervous since I haven't been with anyone but Kurt in over twenty years. But…"

"But what?"

"You make me feel safe."

"Good," he said and kissed her forehead. "Do you think I should leave before they all get home?"

Liv thought, *I can't believe a year ago, I was in this same bed in this same house with Kurt. How would Austin feel about all of this?* She sat up. The moonlight was streaming through the windows and she could hear the crashing surf. She took Chase's hand and kissed it.

"Chase, I want you to stay here with me more than anything. But I'm worried about how my children might feel, especially Austin."

"Liv, Don't worry. I completely understand," said Chase. He stood up and began getting dressed.

"I'll walk you out," said Liv.

When they reached the front door, Chase kissed her again. "Sleep well," he said.

"You, too. See you tomorrow."

"I can't wait." He kissed her one more time and then she closed the door.

Liv climbed into bed, reliving the evening in her mind. Soon, she received a text: *Liv, thank you for an unforgettable evening. I'll text you in the morning. Sweet dreams, Chase XO.*

Liv smiled and texted back. *Sweet dreams, XOXO.* She rolled over, placed her phone on the nightstand, and felt completely at peace, something she hadn't felt in months. "Thank you, God," she said, and then drifted off to sleep.

CHAPTER 10

The Perfect Day

The next morning, Liv woke up to a quiet house. She made herself a cup of coffee and stepped out onto the balcony. The ocean was wild, and Liv could see dark clouds building over the horizon.

Liv quickly finished her coffee and threw on her workout clothes, hoping to get her beach walk in before the rain started. Just as she was about to leave, Amanda and Rose came out of their bedrooms.

"So, how was your friendly dinner?" asked Amanda.

"Let's just say it wasn't terrible," Liv smiled. "And maybe you were right."

"I knew it! Okay, I want to hear everything."

"Amanda, I promise to tell you all about it, but I really want to go for my morning walk before it starts raining."

"Okay, but just promise to give me all of the juicy details as soon as you get back."

"You got it."

And with that, Liv was out the door. After about thirty minutes into her walk, she received a text. *Good morning, XO.*

It was from Chase. Liv stopped and took a picture of the stormy sky over the ocean and sent it to him, replying, *Good morning, Chase, XOXO.*

As soon as she sent the message, her phone rang.

"Good morning, Liv. You're out on your walk, I see."

"Yes, I'm trying to beat the rain."

"How did you sleep last night?"

Liv laughed. "I haven't slept that well in years, if you must know."

"Me, too. So what's the plan for today?"

"I'm not sure. No one was up when I left, except for Amanda and Rose. And I'm sure the boys are sleeping off their bingo fun from last night."

"No doubt," laughed Chase. "Well, listen, I'd really like to see you today."

"I'd like to see you, too. Oh, and by the way, we're all going to the Barn for dinner since it's our last night on the island. And I was hoping you'd join us."

"Of course. I'd love to come," Chase said. "Bennie's Red Barn, I assume? And let me guess—it's another family tradition."

"You guessed it."

"Well, you can definitely count me in. But please give me a call when you get back to the house and let me know what the day's plans look like."

"Chase Montgomery, are you missing me?"

Chase laughed. "I guess you've figured me out already. And if you must know, I'm counting the seconds until I get to see that beautiful smile of yours again."

"Well, handsome, I promise not to keep you waiting much longer. In fact, I'm heading back now. Oh, boy, I just saw a huge bolt of lightning."

"Okay, Liv. Stay safe. And call me when you get back."

"Don't worry, I will." Liv hung up and put her phone into a Ziploc bag and started heading back towards the house, but she'd only gone a few steps before the storm rolled in over the island. The rain was heavy with strong gusts of wind. Loud claps of thunder rang out over the ocean and Liv was getting pelted by the raindrops.

Forty minutes later, she was finally back at the cottage, soaked to the bone. She grabbed a warm towel out of the dryer and then walked into the living room where all of the boys were laid out on the sofas and chairs watching ESPN.

"Wow, look at you, Love," said Beau.

"The heavy stuff isn't coming down for a while," Liv laughed. "So, no breakfast this morning, Beau?"

"No, Love, Bingo kicked my ass. But don't get me wrong. It was a great evening. I just had way too many martinis."

William started laughing. "Mom, you should've seen Beau out on the dance floor. I think he danced with every woman there."

"I think I did, too," said Beau.

"Guess what, Mom," said Jeffrey. "I won $500 last night."

"Wow, Jeffrey, that's awesome."

"So, Mom, how was dinner?" asked Austin.

"Really fun," Liv replied. "And the food was over the top. So listen, what are we all going to do on this rainy day?"

"I say we head over to the gym and sweat out all of this alcohol," said Austin.

"Great idea," agreed William. "I think we also need to hit the steam room. After that, let's go to Barbara Jean's for a hangover brunch."

"Sounds like a plan," said Beau.

"I'll text Chase and see if he wants to join us," said William.

"I just did," said Austin. "He can't. He's going to Sunday service with his grandparents and then they're heading over to Jekyll Island for brunch."

He is? Liv thought to herself. *Funny he didn't mention any of that to me on the phone.*

"Can Rose and I come to brunch?" Amanda asked.

"Sure," said William. "And then let's all go see the new *Star Wars* movie."

"Perfect," said Beau. "A dark movie theater is just what I need."

"Okay, but please don't forget about dinner tonight," said Liv. "We have to be at the Barn at 6:30."

"We're going to dinner in a barn?" asked Beau.

"Yes," said Austin. "We go every year."

"Don't worry, Beau, you're going to love it," said Liv.

"What are you going to do today, Mom?" asked William. "Do you want to come to brunch?"

"No, I think I'll stay here and start packing up for the drive home tomorrow."

"Okay, if you're sure."

"I'm sure. I'm going to go take a hot shower and get out of these wet clothes."

As soon as Liv stepped out of the shower, her cell phone rang. She wrapped a towel around herself and answered.

"Hey, beautiful," said Chase on the other end. "Austin texted me and told me what the plans are for today. So what are you going to do?"

"I'm just going to spend the day packing," said Liv. "Chase, are you really going to Sunday service with your grandparents and over to Jekyll Island for brunch?"

"Oh no, I just told Austin that. I was actually hoping to spend the day with you, if that's okay. I thought maybe I could swing by and pick you up around 1:00."

"Sure, I guess that would be okay," said Liv.

"Great. I'll see you soon."

"See you soon, handsome."

Liv went around the house picking up sandy beach towels and dirty laundry. She cleaned up the kitchen, then she packed Rose's suitcase and her toys. Just as she began to pack her own suitcase, the doorbell rang. She opened the door and there stood Chase.

"Chase, it's not even 12:30 yet. What are you doing here?"

"Well, I checked the forecast, and the rain is supposed to stop soon. So, I asked the hotel to pack us up a picnic lunch and I thought we could drive over to the lighthouse. What do you think?"

Liv smiled. "Chase, I think it would be very hard to ever say no to you. Now, just let me go change, and then we can head out."

"Oh, please don't change. I think you look perfect. And besides, I left my car running."

"Okay. I'm a bit of a mess, but okay." Liv grabbed her flip flops and beach bag and was out the door.

"Look," Chase said as he put the car's top down. "I told you it was going to stop raining."

Soon they were cruising down Sea Island Road with the sun sparkling off of the marshes. As they drove down Mallory Street, they passed by all of the quaint shops and restaurants the island had to offer. Chase found a parking spot next to the pier. He reached back and grabbed the picnic basket. They walked through Neptune Park and found a picnic table next to the lighthouse. Chase opened the picnic basket and unfolded a tablecloth and then set the table.

"Wow, look at all of this," said Liv.

The hotel had packed for them a cheese plate, finger sandwiches, and deviled eggs, plus a chilled bottle of champagne. Chase opened the champagne and poured them each a glass.

"Cheers to the perfect day," said Liv.

"And to many more," Chase added. He fed Liv a strawberry and then kissed her.

Liv kissed Chase back and then glanced out at the water and said, "Look, Chase, there are three dolphins right out in front of the lighthouse."

"You're right," said Chase. "Hey, after lunch, we can go to the top of the lighthouse if you want."

"I'd like that," said Liv. "But first, come here and kiss me again."

Chase leaned over the table and passionately kissed her. Her stomach did another somersault. After dining on their scrumptious lunch, they decided to walk out onto the pier and then ventured up the 129 steps to the top of the lighthouse. Once at the top, they stepped outside. The view was magnificent. They could see Jekyll Island, Brunswick, and the south end of St. Simons. Chase put his arm around Liv as they both marveled at the scenery.

"Thank you," said Liv.

"For what?"

"I haven't been this happy in a very long time."

Chase smiled and kissed her.

When they returned to the car, Chase said, "So do you want to head back now?"

"No, not yet," said Liv. "There's still one more place I'd like to go."

"Okay. Where to?"

"Christ Church. I haven't been there in years and it would mean a lot to me." Back when Kurt had proposed to Liv, she had suggested that they get married at Christ Church. Nestled under huge live oaks and cedar trees, Christ Church was a perfect, little, white wooden chapel that had been built in 1820. But Kurt was appalled by the idea of getting married in such a simple church.

"Sure," said Chase. "Let's go."

Soon, they were driving down Frederica Road and heading towards the church. As they turned the bend, the Spanish moss once again made a canopy over the road. And as the small, white chapel came into view, Chase slowed the car down until it came to a complete stop.

"Chase, what are you doing?" asked Liv.

"Come here and kiss me," Chase replied. He leaned over and kissed Liv under the canopy of trees. Then he drove on and parked the car in front of the church and came around to open Liv's door.

The church was just as Liv had remembered it. Chase slid his hand into Liv's as they walked past the cemetery. He took out his phone and began to take pictures of the headstones, some of which dated back to the 1700s. He also took pictures of Liv as she walked down the stone path under the oak trees toward the front door of the church.

They seemed to be the only ones on the church grounds that day. "Should we go in?" asked Liv.

"I'm sure it's locked," said Chase as he looked around. Liv pulled on the white double doors and, much to her surprise, the door opened. They stepped quietly inside and walked down the red carpet toward the altar. The wooden, Gothic, arched ceiling took on a magical glow from the candles that were lit on the altar, as the afternoon sunlight came streaming through the stained-glass windows.

"Why are the candles lit?" whispered Liv.

"I'm not sure," answered Chase.

"I'd like to pray, if that's okay."

Chase nodded his head. They both walked up to the front of the church and sat down at the first pew on the right. Liv kneeled and Chase did the same, reaching out and taking Liv's hand. Liv bowed her head and closed her eyes, silently praying, *"Dear Lord, thank you for all of my many blessings. Thank you for my amazing children. Thank you for the love and support of my family. Dear God, I need your help. This has been such a very difficult time for all of us, please give me the strength to get through this, and I do pray that one day I will find love again. Amen."*

Liv looked at Chase. He smiled. They stood up, and walked out of the church's side door. As soon as they stepped outside, the sun peeked out from behind the clouds. Chase kissed Liv, and then looked deeply into her eyes. "Liv, I see my future when I look into your eyes."

Liv said nothing, but she had to admit that she felt exactly the same way. And On this dreamy, tiny island in Georgia, Olivia Whittaker had magically found love once again.

CHAPTER 11

Under the Georgia Sky

That evening at 6:30, Liv and her children carried on one of their favorite family traditions by having their last supper on the island in Bennie's Red Barn. When they arrived at the Barn, they posed for group photos with the Barn's giant wagon wheel as the backdrop. After their photo session, the hostess showed them to their usual round table in the corner of the restaurant, next to the bar.

Beau sat back and soaked in the history of the Barn. The Barn had been serving locals and tourists on the island since 1954. The decor was red-and-white-checkered tablecloths, oil lanterns, and stuffed wildlife that was hung on the walls and rafters. There were no menus. The waitstaff, who had all been there for decades, rattled off the dinner items and daily specials, so you needed to pay close attention.

After much deliberation, the group placed their appetizers and dinner orders, which included conch fritters, shrimp and oyster cocktails, the Barn's award-winning fried chicken, broiled seafood platters with sides of sherried mushrooms, fried okra and succotash, and, for dessert, their over-the-top homemade pecan pie.

As they all sat enjoying their last meal together on the island in this unforgettable setting, Beau raised his wine glass to make a toast.

"I would just like to say thank you all for having me on this amazing trip. And I really hope I get invited back next year." They all clinked glasses.

"Here's to next year," said Austin.

"Well, maybe next year Beau won't drink so many margaritas at Bubba Garcia's and lose his wallet," laughed William.

"Beau, I still can't believe you lost your wallet and driver's license," said Liv.

"I don't know what to say, Love," said Beau. "This island makes you do crazy things."

Ain't that the truth, thought Liv. She glanced across the table at Chase who winked and smiled back at her. Liv wondered how her sons would feel if they knew that Chase and she had slept together. But because everyone was getting along so nicely, Liv felt that there was no reason to rock the boat at this point. And besides, she thought, this island truly does possess magical powers. *Maybe once we're back home, whatever has been going on between Chase and me will simply fizzle out.*

Just then the waitress appeared with their pecan pies.

"Mommy, I need to use the bathroom," said Rose.

"Okay, I'll take you," said Liv. As Liv was helping Rose wash her hands in the restroom, she received a text message: *Liv, I really need to speak to you alone tonight. Please meet me down on the beach at ten. It's important, Chase.*

Liv wondered what Chase needed to see her about, but texted back, *Okay, I'll be there.*

When Liv got back to the table she nervously glanced over at Chase and smiled. "So, before we head back to the house," she said, "I just wanted to thank you all for helping to keep our Sea Island tradition alive. Cheers!"

Once they had returned to the cottage, Liv pulled Amanda aside. "Amanda, look at this text," she said, showing her Chase's text message.

"Wow," said Amanda. "I wonder what he's going to tell you. Maybe he's going to confess his undying love for you!"

"Listen, Amanda, that's not funny. I really want to keep this all quiet for now. So I'm definitely going to need your help."

"Okay, what do you want me to do?"

"After I put Rose to bed, I'm going to say goodnight to everyone and then sneak out of my bedroom door onto the balcony so I can meet Chase down on the beach. Now, if for some reason they figure out I'm gone, please text me."

"You got it, but they're all super exhausted, so I really don't think you have anything to worry about."

"Well, let's hope you're right."

"Besides, you worry too much. Just go and have fun."

"Amanda, Sneaking out at my age isn't exactly fun anymore."

"Well, you could have fooled me," laughed Amanda. "Liv, be honest, hasn't this been a great vacation? You have two gorgeous men fighting over you."

"All right, Amanda, that's enough. Now, let's go and get Rose ready for bed."

After Rose was tucked in for the night, Liv went out into the living room. Everyone had gone to bed except for Beau, Austin, and William.

"Well, I'm going to head off to bed now," said Liv. "Beau, I really want to be on the road by ten tomorrow morning, if that's okay with you?"

"Sure, Love," Beau replied as he stood up from the couch. He put his arms around her. "Thanks again for an incredible trip. I'm beat, fellas, I'll see you all in the morning." Then Beau kissed Liv on the cheek and headed down the hallway to his bedroom.

Liv turned to Austin and William. "Sleep well, boys, and don't stay up too late."

"Okay, Mom. Good night," said Austin and William.

Liv turned and went into her bedroom, picked up her phone, and sent Chase a text message: *Heading down to the beach now.*

Moments later, Chase replied: *Me too.*

Liv's heart was pounding as she opened her bedroom door and stepped out onto the balcony. She carefully climbed over the railing and quickly crossed the lawn and then headed down to the beach. It was pitch black except for the full moon reflecting brilliantly off of the ocean.

Where is he? She took out her phone and sent him a text: *Chase, I'm on the beach. Where are you?*

Look for the flashlight on my phone. I'm down in front of the beach club, Chase replied.

Liv looked down the beach and saw a small light heading in her direction. She began walking quickly toward the light. When she finally reached Chase, he was holding a blanket and a beach bag.

"Chase, what is this all about?"

Chase spread the blanket out onto the sand. "Liv, please sit down," he said. Liv nervously sat down. Next, Chase pulled out a split of champagne and two plastic champagne flutes. He opened the bottle and poured them each a glass.

Liv put her glass down and said, "Chase, we need to talk."

"Oh, boy," said Chase. "That doesn't sound good."

"Well, it's just that maybe we both got caught up with the romance and the magic of this beautiful island. Chase, what I'm trying to say is that I think we both have some serious thinking to do when we get home. Also, I don't know how my boys would feel about me dating you. And what about your friendship with Austin. Have you even thought about that? And, Chase, let's not forget, I'm not even divorced yet. And one more thing—Doesn't

79

our age difference bother you? You must want to be with someone your own age."

"First of all," Chase replied, "our age difference doesn't bother me at all. I want you, Liv. And, yes, I understand your concerns about the boys, but at the end of the day, I would hope your sons, including Austin, would want to see their mother in a happy, loving relationship."

Then Chase reached into the beach bag and pulled out a small box. He handed it to Liv. "Open it."

Liv slowly opened the box. Inside was a gold, sideways cross necklace. Chase took it out of the box and put it around Liv's neck. "I saw it in the hotel's gift shop and it made me think of you. Liv, I want this necklace to be a symbol of my feelings for you and the time we've shared on this island. I want us both to remember how we felt that afternoon at the church." Then he leaned over and kissed her. "And because we're both in a difficult situation, I think we should just keep the feelings we have for each other between us for now."

He leaned over and kissed her again. Then he lay down on his back. "Come here, Liv." Liv lay down next to him. "Would you look at all of those stars?" Liv looked up at the billions of stars in the Georgia sky on that July night. She leaned over and kissed him.

"Chase," she said.

"Yes?"

"I want to tell you something."

Chase sat up and said, "Okay. Liv, What is it?"

Liv sat next to him and held his hand. "It's about the other night."

"Oh, my gosh, are you sorry that we slept together? Was it too soon? Oh, God, this is all my fault. You weren't ready."

"Chase, the other night was amazing. It was…it was…"

"It was what?"

"Okay, so this is very hard for me to say and I'm actually super embarrassed."

"Liv, please just tell me."

"Well, I just wanted you to know that my sex life with Kurt had become very mechanical and routine over the last few years. And also, sex was always about pleasing him, if you know what I mean. So, the other night with you was incredibly special to me." Liv kissed Chase's hand. "I just thought you should know."

Chase tucked Liv's hair behind her ear and said, "It was special to me, too. And I love pleasing you, Liv. And if you'll let me, I want to continue to please you in every way." Then he gently kissed her.

"Chase, you made me remember how good it can be."

"So you liked it?" Chase said with a devilish grin.

"Yes, Chase," she whispered in his ear. "I loved it."

"Well then, may I have you again here tonight on this beach?"

"Yes, Chase, I want to remember this night and the way you make me feel always."

Chase lay down on his side and pulled Liv close to him. He began kissing her and then he reached down and pulled his shirt up over his head. Liv stood up and removed her dress. Chase slid off his pants and then stood up next to her, two naked silhouettes in the moonlight.

"Lay down," she said. Chase lay down on his back and Liv straddled him. She closed her eyes as he slid inside of her. *My God, I love the way he feels*, she thought. She never remembered anyone feeling as good as he did. He reached up and flipped her over onto her back. He began touching her.

"I want you inside of me," she whispered.

He leaned down and kissed her as he slid back inside of her. She looked up into his beautiful eyes and wished that they could stay just like this forever. And at that moment, they both climaxed.

Afterwards, they lay in each other's arms with their hands intertwined, and Liv knew in her heart that this romance was far from over. *No*, she thought, *this romance has just begun, here on a summer's night under the Georgia sky.*

CHAPTER 12

Forbidden Fruit

The next morning, Beau, Rose, and Liv were headed home. As they drove down Sea Island Drive, Liv rolled down her window. She wanted to soak in every last second of being on the island. And because she had no idea what her finances were going to look like next year or for the years to come, she was afraid that this could possibly be her last trip to the island.

When they turned onto the ramp for I-95 south, Beau reached over and grabbed Liv's hand. "You're awfully quiet this morning, Love."

"Just call it the Sea Island blues," sighed Liv.

"Are you sure there isn't more to it?"

"Like what?"

"Like your love affair with Chase Montgomery?"

Liv stared out the window not quite knowing what to say.

"It's obvious, you know," said Beau. "The way you two look at each other. Neither one of you is hiding it very well. Also, the night that we all went to bingo, I left the ballroom for a bit to go and check on you. And when I walked past the Georgian Room Lounge, I saw the two of you dancing."

Oh, God, Liv thought. "I'm so sorry, Beau."

83

"Me too, Love. But don't be sorry for me. You're the one who's going to end up with a broken heart."

"What are you talking about?"

"Have you really thought about what a mess this is? Love, let me fill you in. First off, he's much too young for you."

"Beau, he's only two years younger than you are."

"Love, Let me finish," said Beau. "There is no way Arthur and Birdie Montgomery will ever accept you into their family. Chase is their only child. Love, they're going to want him to carry on the Montgomery name."

"So what? I can still have more children."

"Are you insane? And please forgive me for saying this, but you can hardly manage the four you have now. Not to mention what a huge health risk that would be for you. Love, all I'm trying to say is that the last thing you need is another child."

"Damn you, Beau, you're talking to me like I'm a hundred years old or something!"

"Hey, don't get mad at me, I'm just pointing out the obvious. And speaking of children, how do you think Austin is going to feel about someone that he has looked up to his whole life fucking his mother?"

"That's enough, Beau. I mean it."

"Love, I'm telling you, this has disaster written all over it. So, please take my advice and end this before everyone gets hurt."

Liv reached up and touched her cross necklace, not knowing how to respond. Finally, she said, "Beau, I appreciate your advice, but believe me, I know what I'm doing."

"Okay, then. I've said my piece. But just know when this whole thing blows up in your face, I'll still be the man sitting right beside you. Chase will leave. He doesn't have the stomach to deal with this mess, and in the end, he'll choose his family. Trust me, you'll see, but just remember, I warned you."

Liv turned around and was thankful that Rose was sound asleep in the backseat. She glanced down at her watch. In three hours They would be home. *I think this is going to be the longest car ride of my life,* she thought.

CHAPTER 13

Second Thoughts

At 6:00 a.m., after tossing and turning all night, Liv finally decided to go downstairs to make her morning coffee. She couldn't get her conversation with Beau out of her head. On her way to the kitchen, she walked past the dining room and noticed the stacks of mail and bills that were piled up on the table.

She made her coffee and then went into the library where she turned on the family computer. As she was going through her emails, she felt completely overwhelmed. Her cell phone buzzed with a text message: *Liv, welcome home, Chase. XO.*

She stared at the phone unsure how to answer. *Chase, we need to talk, she wrote back.*

Her phone rang immediately.

"Good morning, Liv. Is everything okay?"

"Not really," she replied. "There are huge stacks of bills on the dining room table. And, Chase, I'm embarrassed to say this, but I haven't paid a bill in over twenty years. Kurt always took care of all of our bills, and, if I'm being completely honest, I'm not even sure where to begin."

"Liv, There's no need to worry. I'm sure I can set up auto-pay for most of your bills. And also, I would be happy to outline a household budget for you, if you'd like."

"You'd do that for me?"

"Of course, I would. Listen, why don't I come over after work today?"

Liv didn't know what to say.

"Liv, is anything else bothering you?" asked Chase.

"Well, to be honest, I'm just wondering if we're doing the right thing."

"What do you mean?"

"I'm talking about us, Chase. I'm thinking maybe we should stop all of this before someone gets hurt."

"Look, Liv, you just got home and you're clearly feeling overwhelmed. I think we should just take things one day at a time for now. I'll tell you what. Why don't I pick up some steaks and a nice bottle of wine after work. I can be over at your house around six. What do you say?"

Liv finally gave in and said, "Okay, Chase."

"And, Liv, please stop worrying. Everything is going to be fine, I promise. Now, I hope you have a good day, and I'll see you tonight."

"See you tonight."

That evening at six sharp, Chase pulled into Liv's driveway. He came into the house carrying grocery bags and a bouquet of sunflowers. Chase handed her the flowers and kissed her. "So where is everyone?" he asked.

"Jeffrey and William have to work late tonight, Rose is swimming in the pool, and Austin's on a date with one of the waitresses from HMF."

"So it's just us and Rose tonight?"

"Yes," Liv said nervously as she put the sunflowers in a vase.

"Great. Well, I'll go fire up the grill. And then after dinner, we can go through your bills."

Once again, Chase impressed Liv with his cooking skills. "Thanks so much for making us dinner," she said.

"Liv, you know I love cooking for you and Rose."

Rose got up and gave Chase a big hug.

"Rose," said Liv, "if you're finished with your dinner, you can go change into your pajamas and put the TV on for a little while before bedtime. Chase and I are going to clean up and do some work in the library." And with that, Rose ran into the house.

Liv and Chase cleared their dinner plates and loaded the dishwasher. "I'll be right back," said Chase. "I forgot something in my car." Chase returned with a stack of colored folders, all of which he had already labeled: auto insurance, home insurance, mortgage, taxes, credit cards, etc.

"What's all this?" asked Liv.

"Well, first we're going to organize your bills into these folders. After that, I can see which ones I can set up for you on auto-pay and then we'll go from there." They began sorting and filing all of Liv's bills. Then Chase went to work on the computer, setting up auto-pay and an easy filing system for Liv. At around midnight, they were finally finished.

"Chase, I really can't thank you enough. You have definitely lifted a huge weight off of my shoulders."

"It was a breeze. But, Liv, I do have some concerns. Your monthly expenses are over $25,000. You can't be expected to carry all of this on your own. Kurt should be paying for at least half, if not more."

"I know, Chase. And you're right. I actually spoke with my attorney today and she assured me that Kurt will be forced to reimburse me at the time of our mediation."

"Okay, well, that's a bit of good news, at least. So, are you feeling a little better than you did this morning?"

Liv looked down, once again not knowing what to say. Chase stepped closer toward her.

"Liv, look at me. What's going on?"

Liv looked up at him with tears in her eyes. "That's the thing," she said. "I'm not sure."

He leaned in and kissed her. "Liv, We don't have to figure this all out tonight. Just promise me you'll give us a chance."

"Okay," Liv nodded.

"So I was thinking that we should go away together for a night. I want to enjoy another beautiful dinner with you, I want to spend the night making love to you, and the next morning wake up with you lying next to me. Liv, Please don't say no."

Liv looked into those beautiful green-blue eyes, and there was no way she could say no.

"Okay, but just for one night," she said. "And I have no idea what I'm going to tell my children."

"Liv, You don't have to figure this all out on your own. I'm here and I'm not going anywhere."

"Promise?"

"Promise." Then Chase kissed her again.

CHAPTER 14

"Fuck You, Kurt!"

July 13th, 2015. Liv was in her bedroom packing for her romantic overnight getaway with Chase. She decided to tell her children that she was going away for the night with her best friend Lisa for a girls' trip down to Miami. She felt terrible about lying to them, but she knew she had no other option. She needed to spend some more time alone with Chase to see if her feelings for him were real or just the product of a romantic vacation.

She went into her closet and opened her lingerie drawer. She thought to herself, *I wonder which one of these Chase would like the best?* Just then she remembered she had forgotten to book the car service. Even though Chase and Liv were staying in Palm Beach, Chase thought it would be best if they hired a car service for the twenty-four hours that they'd be away. He wanted them to be as discreet as possible.

Liv picked up her phone and dialed A1A Limo. Kurt and Liv had used them for years and they were always very reliable.

"Yes, hi, this is Mrs. Donovan," she said when the receptionist answered.

"Hi, Mrs. Donovan. How can I help you today?"

"I would like to schedule a twenty-four-hour car service, please."

"Okay, I'd be happy to help you with that. Do you have an account with us?"

"Yes, I do."

"Can I please have your phone number?"

"Sure." Liv recited her phone number.

"Okay, I see you in our system. Are we picking you up at your home at 145 Seaspray Avenue?"

"Yes," said Liv. "And, also, I was hoping to book a sedan."

"Of course, no problem. What will be the date and time of the pick-up?"

"July 16th at 1:00 p.m., please."

"And where will you be heading to?"

"Well, first, we need to make a quick stop to pick up my friend, and then we'll be heading over to the Chesterfield Hotel."

"Okay. Can I please have your friend's name and address?"

"His name is Chase Montgomery, and he lives at 134 Chilean Avenue."

"Okay, Mrs. Donovan. Let me read this back to you. We're going to be picking you up at your home on July 16th at 1:00 p.m. and then we are going over to 134 Chilean Avenue to pick up Mr. Montgomery, and dropping you both off at the Chesterfield Hotel. And you would like the driver and car to be at your disposal for twenty-four hours. Is that correct?"

"Yes."

"Okay, you're all set and we'll see you in a couple days."

"Great," said Liv. "And thank you."

Liv hung up the phone and went back to her packing. The next day, when she was driving to the Eau Spa to get a manicure and pedicure, her cell phone rang. She dug through her purse, found her phone, and answered. The voice on the other end said, "Liv, have you lost your fucking mind?!"

Oh, God, it's Kurt!

Kurt continued. "I just got a call from A1A Limo to confirm your reservation, which includes picking up Chase fucking Montgomery and checking into the Chesterfield Hotel! Olivia, may I remind you that you are still legally my wife?! I will not allow you to be running all over our town with your new boy toy and screwing him in a hotel. Do you understand me, Olivia? I won't stand for it!"

Liv pulled into the closest parking lot. She was shaking.

"Kurt, I may still be your wife on paper, but not for long. And by the way, you no longer have the right to say where I go, what I do, and who I sleep with! Fuck you, Kurt!"

And with that, she hung up. She closed her eyes and took a deep breath. She then decided to call Chase. When he answered, she recapped her conversation with Kurt.

"Chase, maybe we shouldn't go away," she said.

"No, Liv, we're going," replied Chase.

"Well, maybe we should go somewhere else," said Liv. "He knows where we're staying."

"Who the fuck cares, Liv?! He walked out on you and the kids. And on top of that, you've hardly even heard from him. Look, I'm sorry, I didn't mean to raise my voice at you. And if you really don't want to go, I'll respect that."

Liv stared out of her car window. "No, I *do* want to go. I was just taken off guard by his phone call. And Chase, I know you only met Kurt a handful of times, but trust me, he can be extremely intimidating."

"Liv, like I said, I'm okay with whatever you want to do.

"Chase, I want to go."

"Are you sure?"

"Yes, Chase, I'm very sure. And besides, I've been looking forward to it all week."

"Okay. So, we're going?"

"Yes, Chase, we're going."

"Great. I'll give you a call on my way home from work."

"Sounds good. I'll talk to you later." She then hung up the phone and prayed she was doing the right thing.

CHAPTER 15

A Night to Remember

Afew days later, Liv was out on her front porch waiting for the car service to arrive. Luckily, Ms. Dee had agreed to stay the night to look after Rose and the house. The boys were all at work, and so far, no one had suspected a thing.

At 1:00 p.m. sharp, a stretch limo pulled into the driveway. *What on earth?* she thought. She walked toward the car with her suitcase. The driver, Carl, immediately ran across the driveway to assist her. Liv knew Carl very well. He had driven Liv many times over the past few years.

"Carl, what is all this?" Liv said. "I asked for a sedan."

"I know, Mrs. Donovan," Carl replied, "but Mr. Donovan called our office and went nuts. So, at that point, the secretary realized she confirmed your trip with the wrong person, which was a huge mistake on our part. John, the owner, hopes you'll accept his apology. And of course, there will be no charge for the twenty-four hour service."

"Carl, this is truly embarrassing. Kurt and I are getting divorced."

"Mrs. Donovan, say no more. I've been with this company for over twenty years now and believe me when I tell you I've seen it all. So, shall we be on our way?"

Carl opened the back door to the limo and Liv climbed on in. In less than five minutes, they pulled up to Chase's guest house. Chase walked toward the limo with his suitcase, wearing navy dress pants, a white button-down, and his Ferragamo loafers, with a matching belt. Liv rolled down her window.

"Do you need a lift, handsome?"

Chase laughed. "Liv, What is this?"

"Get in, gorgeous, and I'll explain everything."

Chase followed Carl around to the trunk to put in his luggage. Then he climbed into the back of the limo with Liv and soon they were on their way.

"Liv, so what happened to us being discreet?" Chase asked.

"Well, A1A felt bad about the mix-up with Kurt, so they decided to give us an upgrade. Also, there's no charge for the service."

"Liv, that's very nice of them, but we might as well be driving around town with a huge sign that says, 'Liv and Chase are sleeping together.'"

Liv rolled her eyes and laughed. "Kiss me."

Chase leaned over and gave Liv a passionate kiss.

Just then, the car stopped suddenly.

"Now what?" asked Liv. "Chase, why are we pulled over on Worth Avenue?"

"Liv, don't worry, we're just making a quick stop before heading over to the hotel," said Chase.

Carl hopped out and opened Liv's door. Chase came around and took her hand as she stepped out of the limo.

"Chase, why are we in front of Tiffany's?" Liv asked.

"Come on, Liv. I have a little surprise for you."

As Chase held open the door to the jewelry store, Liv suddenly felt very uncomfortable. She had been in Tiffany's many times with

Kurt over the years, and she immediately spotted her favorite salesgirl walking towards her.

"Hi, Jane," said Liv. "It's so nice to see you again."

"You as well, Olivia. How are the children?"

"Fine, thanks."

"So Chase has a very thoughtful surprise for you today."

"Oh, I didn't realize that you two knew each other."

"We didn't until he came in two days ago and arranged this special day for you. Now, if you two will just follow me into one of our private showrooms…"

"Wait," said Liv. Then, turning to Chase, she said. "Can I speak to Jane alone for a moment?"

"Of course," Chase replied. "I'll be over at the men's watches."

"I'm sorry, Jane," said Liv after Chase had walked away.

"Olivia, there's nothing to be sorry about," said Jane. "I was certainly sad and surprised to hear about your divorce, but I understand that these things happen. And, by the way, it looks like you found yourself a real winner. What Chase has planned for you today is incredibly sweet. So, shall we go into the showroom now?"

Liv nodded and waved Chase back over. They followed Jane into the private room where Jane poured them each a glass of champagne.

"I'll be right back," she said, and then she slipped out of the room.

"Chase, What's going on?" Liv asked.

"Don't worry," said Chase. "I'm pretty sure you're going to like it." Then he leaned over and kissed her.

Jane returned with a large, black velvet tray that held at least a dozen rings. "I'll give you two some time alone," she said as she placed the tray onto the table and then closed the door behind her.

"Chase, what's going on?" asked Liv.

"Well, I know how upset you've been about having to turn over your jewelry to the attorneys, so I thought it would be nice to get you a new ring to celebrate the start of your new life."

"Chase, I'm sorry, but this is way too much. We haven't been dating each other long enough for you to be buying me such an expensive gift."

"Liv, please let me do this for you. It would mean a lot to me. Now, which one do you like?" Chase began picking up the rings one by one and sliding them onto Liv's finger. After trying them all on, they both agreed on the Tiffany's "Enchant" heart-shaped ring in platinum with diamonds.

Liv held up her hand to admire the ring, "It's perfect, Chase. I love it."

He took her finger and said, "If you look closely, there are two diamonds in the middle, and the side of the heart reminds me of the waves in the ocean."

"Yes, this is definitely the one."

"Okay, great. I'll go and tell Jane."

When they were back in the limo, Liv looked down at the ring and then looked at Chase. "Chase, thank you. I'm never taking it off."

He reached down and touched the ring. "I'm so glad you like it." He leaned over and gave her another romantic kiss.

The car pulled to a slow stop in front of the Chesterfield Hotel. Carl opened the back door to the limo and the bellman appeared to help with the luggage.

At the reservation desk, the receptionist asked, "Are you checking in?"

"Yes, last name is Montgomery," Chase replied.

"Okay, yes," the receptionist said, "I see your reservation right here. Mr. and Mrs. Montgomery. We have you checking into our one-bedroom suite for one night." As Chase handed him his credit card, he detailed the hotel amenities.

97

"The hotel's pool is down the hall on your left, along with the outdoor bar, which is open tonight until 7:00 p.m. Also, we'll be serving afternoon tea in the Leopard Lounge at 4:00. This evening, we also have live music and dinner in there as well. The Courtyard Restaurant serves breakfast, lunch, and dinner daily. Here are your room keys, sir, and I'll have the bellman show you to your room."

"Thank you," replied Chase.

Liv and Chase followed the bellman through the small, elegant lobby, which housed the largest display of roses that Liv had ever seen. Liv stopped to admire them. "Are these all real?" she asked as she touched one.

"Yes, miss," said the bellman. "They're actually petrified roses. They'll never die and they'll never lose their scent." The bellman carefully pulled a rose from the display and handed it to Liv.

Liv smelled the rose. "Amazing. Thank you."

They then all entered a very small elevator with a hand-painted door showing a large palm tree with a monkey hanging from it.

"How old is the hotel?" asked Liv.

"The hotel dates back to 1926," the bellman replied. "It's changed hands a few times over the years but, thankfully, its charm remains the same. By the way, you two should really check out the Leopard Lounge tonight. It's definitely a must, and don't forget to look up at the ceiling."

"The ceiling?"

"Yes, it's all hand-painted and the murals are quite interesting."

The elevator stopped on the third floor and the bellman walked Chase and Liv to their suite.

"Here we are, room 342." He unlocked the door and brought in their luggage. "As you can see, we have the champagne and strawberries as you had requested. Will you be needing anything else?"

"No, I think we're good," said Chase, handing the bellman a tip.

"Thank you, sir. I hope you both enjoy your stay," said the bellman as he closed the door behind him.

Chase walked over to the coffee table and opened the champagne. He handed Liv a flute and they touched glasses.

"I'm so glad we're finally alone," he said, pulling Liv close and kissing her.

"Chase, what time is our dinner reservation?" asked Liv.

"Seven."

"By the way, handsome, you still haven't told me where we're going tonight."

"Well, I wanted it to be a surprise, but I guess I can tell you now. We're going to Renato's."

Liv took a big sip of champagne. "Chase, why did you choose Renato's?"

"Because I remembered how you said Kurt ruined your birthday last year, and you didn't get to go there. And, you also told me it's your favorite restaurant on the island."

"I see," said Liv, taking another sip of champagne.

"Liv, I was just trying to make a new memory at your favorite restaurant. But if you'd rather go somewhere else, I'm happy to change the reservation."

"No, Chase, that was incredibly thoughtful of you, and I know we'll have a beautiful dinner there. So, Chase, what should we do in the meantime? Do you want to go down to the pool?"

Chase shook his head no.

"Afternoon tea?"

Again, Chase shook his head.

"A walk down Worth Avenue?"

Once more, Chase shook his head.

Liv smiled and walked over to her suitcase where she pulled out red lace lingerie and then slipped into the bathroom. When she returned, Chase was lying on the bed wearing nothing except his black Calvin Klein briefs. Liv lay down on the bed next to him.

"So, what *do* you want to do this afternoon, Mr. Montgomery?" she said with a devilish smile.

"Well, I thought, perhaps, I'd like to do *you*." He grabbed her and pulled her close to him. He then moved gently down her body, kissing every curve along the way. He bit down on her lace thong and with his teeth, slowly dragging it off of her. He started kissing her between her legs. She began to moan quietly. He slowly stuck his tongue inside of her and began touching her to arouse her.

"Do you like it?"

"Yes, it feels amazing."

Liv reached down and touched him. He wanted her.

"I want you inside of me," she whispered.

"I want you to cum for me first."

Every cell in her body was screaming *yes* and then she could feel a warm pool of moisture being released, running down her legs. Chase jumped up on top of her and slid deep inside of her.

"God, I love the way you feel."

"Don't stop!" she screamed. "Please, don't stop!" She wrapped her legs around him as he continued to thrust himself deep inside of her until he exploded. Their drenched bodies clung to each other under the tangled sheets. He was still inside of her and her legs were still wrapped around him.

It had been years since Liv had felt this sensual. Every fiber in her body wanted him. And he knew how to play her body like a beautiful violin.

He started kissing her and smiled. He rolled over and she lay her head on his chest. "Now this is how I would like to spend every afternoon," he said as he made small circles up and down on her arm.

"Me, too," she said, and they both soon drifted off to sleep in each other's arms for a long afternoon nap.

At seven o'clock, Liv and Chase strolled down the Via Mizner flower-bedecked courtyard, reminiscent of old Europe with its cobblestone paths, Mediterranean tiled roofs, and small boutique shops. The sound of the piano being played at Renato's drifted throughout the courtyard.

Chase opened the door for Liv and the host greeted them immediately.

"So good to see you again, Olivia," he said. "It's been too long."

"Yes, it has," said Liv. "I would like you to meet a very dear friend of mine, Chase Montgomery."

"It's a pleasure sir," said the host. "Your usual table is available if you like, Olivia."

"No," said Liv, "I think I'd like to sit somewhere else tonight."

"Well, you can take your pick. It's summer, so we're incredibly slow tonight."

Liv turned to Chase. "Where should we sit?"

"What about the table in the corner that overlooks the courtyard?"

"Excellent choice, sir," said the host, grabbing two menus and the wine list. "Please follow me." At the table, he pulled out Liv's chair and set the menus down. "Enjoy your dinner."

With its breathtaking architecture, intimate dining room, rich fabrics, and warm candlelight, Liv felt that Renato's was one of the most romantic settings she'd ever dined in and was very excited to share the experience with Chase. The sound of the fountain in the courtyard, the chirping birds, along with the bougainvillea trees climbing up the walls reminded Liv of a small, charming village in Italy.

Liv picked up the wine list and handed it to Chase. "I think you should pick the wine tonight. You know what I like," she said with a smile.

He reached over and grabbed her hand. "I want to give you everything you like always," he said as he kissed her hand. He flipped through the wine list and then waved the waiter over. "We'll have a bottle of the Rombauer Chardonnay and also, a bottle of the 1997 Opus One, please."

"Yes, sir," the waiter replied as he removed the wine list.

Chase and Liv looked over their dinner menus and made their selections. "We're going to share the beef carpaccio and Capri salad to start," Chase told the waiter. "And for our main courses, she'll have the wild mushroom pappardelle and I'll have the Ossobuco Milanese."

"Excellent choices, sir," the waiter said. "I'll be right back with your wine and some olive bread."

Liv took her phone out of her purse.

"Is everything all right?" asked Chase.

"Oh, yes, I just want to send a group text to the family and let everyone know that I'm okay." She texted her sons, telling them she'd see them the next day.

Hope you're having fun, Mom, Jeffrey texted back.

Austin and I are heading to dinner with Beau, texted William.

Liv replied, *Please kiss Rose for me. Love you all, Mom.*

She then slid the phone back into her purse.

"Chase, I hate lying to them."

"I know you do, and so do I, but this is a very delicate situation that we're in."

The waiter interrupted to pour the white wine and to decant the red. Chase lifted his wine glass and said, "Cheers to many more romantic dinners." They touched glasses and each took a sip.

Over dinner, Liv began to relax, and once again, she was enjoying getting to know Chase better. She loved how smart he was, his views on world events, and his strong family values. She also loved how he treated her. He made her feel as if she were a precious gift that should be cherished.

"Chase, I have to tell you something," she said over dinner.

"What?"

"I can't find anything wrong with you!"

Chase laughed.

"I'm being serious," Liv continued. "I honestly think you're perfect."

"Well, Liv, I can assure you that I'm far from perfect." He then took her hand. "But do you know what I think?"

"What?" she asked.

"I think we're perfect together." He leaned over and kissed her.

"Chase, this is such a beautiful evening," said Liv. "I never want it to end."

"Well why don't we get the bill and head back to the hotel and check out the Leopard Lounge. Sound good?"

"Sounds perfect."

As they strolled hand in hand back down Coconut Row, the balmy night air surrounded them with the scent of jasmine. And when they entered the Leopard Lounge, they found themselves in a wild scene. The band was in full swing and the dance floor was packed.

Chase went up to the bar and ordered himself a Louis XIII cognac and a glass of Veuve Clicquot for Liv. They found a cozy corner booth and Liv began looking up at the hand-painted red and white ceiling featuring nude figures engaged in interesting, abstract sexual acts.

The piano player began playing "Your Song" by Elton John.

"Do you want to dance?" Chase asked. Liv nodded as he pulled her onto the dance floor. He held her close and began singing to her just as he had done in the Georgia Room lounge. When the song ended, he kissed her. They went on to dance nonstop for the next hour. Finally, Chase said, "Let's head upstairs."

When they got back to the room, Liv looked at Chase and said, "I want you, Chase. I've never wanted anyone the way I want you." Chase started kissing her as he unzipped her dress. She then went and lay down naked on the bed.

"You can do whatever you want to me," she said. "I'm yours."

"Anything?"

"Yes, anything," she whispered.

"Close your eyes."

She closed her eyes. Chase walked over to the ice bucket and placed an ice cube in his mouth. He began running the ice cube over her breast. Her nipples became hard. He then continued down her body. He finally came up and slid what remained of the ice cube into her mouth.

"Are you mine?" he asked.

"Yes. I'm yours."

With that, he slid deep inside of her. She began biting his neck as he moved in and out of her.

"Roll over," she said.

He rolled onto his back and she straddled him. She looked down, loving watching as he slid in and out of her. He was moaning with delight.

"Damn, you feel good," he said.

"I'm yours, remember." She began moving up and down more rapidly, as fast as she could.

He exploded inside of her. She lay her sweaty body on top of his as they both tried to catch their breath. She looked deeply into his eyes. He was still inside of her.

"I love you," he said.

"I love you, too," she replied.

Liv wasn't sure how the future was going to play out between them, but she did know this: it was going to take an army to pry Chase Winston Montgomery IV out of her bed, and especially out of her life.

CHAPTER 16

Meet the Family

Over the next few weeks, Liv and Chase started going out to dinner once a week. They made love any chance they got—on the beach, in the car, in his guest house. And, to put it simply, they just couldn't get enough of each other, but they both agreed to keep their relationship a secret until Liv's divorce was final, which by all accounts would be happening sometime in the fall.

As for Kurt, he was still MIA. Liv's attorney told her that apparently, he was on a super yacht cruising around the French Riviera. This made Liv's blood boil. *He has enough money to go jet-setting around Europe but has yet to give me a single dime to help me support our children,* she thought when she heard of his whereabouts.

Abby Goldstein assured Liv that, eventually, Kurt would have to pay up, but Liv did have another problem hanging over her head. Her boys kept asking, "Mom, when are we going up to Jersey?" Her parents and the rest of the family kept asking as well. She finally confided her concerns to Chase.

"Liv, I don't understand your apprehension," said Chase. "You need your family now more than ever with all that you've been going through."

"I know, Chase, but I don't know how to explain it exactly," said Liv. "I guess I'm just feeling like a failure. All of my cousins are married and have children, so now I'm the odd duck out. Plus, because I married a horrible man, they all had to pitch in and bail me out financially. The whole thing is just terribly embarrassing is all."

"Liv, I really don't think you have anything to worry about. Your family loves you and, so of course, they want to see you and the kids. When were you planning on going?"

"Sometime in August, before Austin and Jeffrey have to head back to school."

"Well, I have to be in New York City the week of August 13th for a Morgan Stanley convention. If you want, I could come down to the shore that following weekend."

"You would do that?"

"Of course. I would love to meet your family, Liv, and see where you grew up."

"But you know I would be introducing you only as a friend, right? Not as my…my…"

"Not as your what, Liv?"

Liv smiled. "Not as my everything."

"Sure, Liv, I understand. We both decided to keep our relationship under wraps for the time being. But I'd still love to meet your family."

"Chase, having you there would mean the world to me."

"So, it's settled then?"

"Well, there's just one other thing," said Liv.

"What's that?"

"So, the boys have already sort of invited Beau."

"What?! Are you kidding me? Look, Liv, I've had to put up with a lot when it comes to Beau Walker—your weekly dinners, daily phone calls. And I know you send him a picture of the ocean every morning on your beach walks, but him flying up to meet your family? Liv, That's just way too much."

"Chase, I realize that you haven't been thrilled with my relationship with Beau. But you can't deny that he has really been here for me and the kids. In fact, he's actually turned into a very dear friend."

"Sure, a very dear friend who would like nothing better than to fuck you."

"Chase! I can't believe you just said that."

"Liv, you know it's true, so please don't even try to deny it."

"Okay, so maybe there are some romantic feelings on his end, but I can assure you that there are none on mine. Look, Chase, I would really love for you to come, but, I'm sorry, I can't tell Beau he's no longer invited."

"Okay," said Chase, "have it your way. But I'm only doing this because I love you so much."

"I know," said Liv, "and I love you, too." She leaned over and kissed him.

"So," said Chase, "I guess I'm going to meet the family."

"I guess you are," she replied as she kissed him again.

CHAPTER 17

Homeward Bound

August 10th, 2015. Liv, Beau, and her children were all standing in the security line at PBI International Airport. For the first time in years, Liv had decided not to travel in a wheelchair. At this point, she felt as though she was strong enough to try and do without it. Also, down the road, she imagined there may come a time in her life when she would have to travel alone. Liv held on tightly to Beau's arm as the line slowly moved. She was feeling dizzy, her heart was pounding, and she felt as though she might faint at any moment.

"Are you okay?" Beau asked. "You look awfully pale."

"Not really," Liv replied, "but I have to do this."

"Are you sure? I can go and grab you a wheelchair."

"No, Beau, I want to try."

"Okay, Love. It's your call."

Beau walked through the metal detector first, followed by Rose, and then Liv.

"Here, Love, come and sit down on this bench," said Beau. He helped her take a seat and then he handed her his ticket and driver's license. "Hold these while I go and grab our things off the security belt."

As he walked away, Liv glanced down at his driver's license. *Good picture*, she thought, and then she looked at the birth date: 2/20/1977. *Wait a minute—1977?* She realized at that moment she wasn't the only one who had been lying about their age. *He's only seven years younger than me*, she thought.

"Here's your purse, Love," said Beau. "Rose, turn around so I can put your backpack on."

Once everyone had gathered up their personal belongings, they all found seats at their gate, and before long, they were able to board the plane.

After settling into their seats in first-class, Beau asked the flight attendant for two glasses of champagne.

"Well, Love we've made it this far," he said when the champagne arrived. "Cheers to another memorable vacation." He and Liv clinked glasses and each took a sip. "Okay, so, tell me again what the plans are for this week."

"Well," Liv replied, "tonight, my parents are having Lenny's Italian Restaurant deliver dinner. Lenny's makes the best pizza at the Jersey Shore hands down. Tomorrow morning, you'll have to get up early because my cousin Roger is going to take you all out fishing for the day. And tomorrow night, my mom is cooking a traditional baked lobster dinner at the house. On Wednesday, I was hoping we could go to lunch over at the Wharfside. It's one of my favorite restaurants at the shore. The food is fantastic, and I'm telling you, the view is to die for. After lunch, I thought we could take Rose up to the boardwalk so she could go on a few rides and play some games. Thursday will just be a relaxing day on the beach. Also, my father told me that the waves are supposed to be good all week, so you can probably go surfing every day if you want. And on Friday, my cousin Brett has set up a tee time for all of you at the Baltusrol Country Club."

"I still can't believe we're going to get to play there," said Beau. "It really is any golfer's dream come true. So, Liv, will Chase be joining us on Friday for golf?"

"Yes, Beau," said Liv.

"Well, this was sounding like the perfect vacation until we got to Friday."

"Beau, please promise me that you'll try to get along with him."

"Love, I give you my word to do my best. But I still think it's a big mistake having him meet your family."

"Well, Beau, he's coming down to the shore and he's meeting my family. And that's that. On Friday night, we're all going to meet up over at the Off Shore Restaurant for dinner. And on Saturday, my mom has arranged for a catered lunch to be served at the house for my entire family. Wow, Beau, I'm exhausted just thinking about the week's events, but I really can't wait to be home. And, Beau, thanks again for coming. I don't think I could have managed today in the airport without you."

"Love, you know I would do anything for you," said Beau.

"I know you would."

Then Beau leaned over and kissed Liv on the cheek. Liv smiled back at him. *I'm finally going home*, she thought.

CHAPTER 18

"Welcome Home, Olivia!"

After a little over two-and-a-half hours, the plane finally touched down at the Newark Liberty International Airport. Liv, Beau, and the children made their way to the baggage claim area where they were greeted by Kevin, the Whittaker's personal driver.

"Welcome home, Olivia!" Kevin said as he gave Liv a huge hug and shook hands with the boys.

"Thanks for coming to get us, Kevin," said Liv.

"No problem at all, you know that."

"Kevin, this is Beau Walker."

"Nice to meet you, Beau," said Kevin, shaking hands with Beau. "And welcome to Jersey."

"Thanks," said Beau.

"Liv, I believe your luggage is coming out over at carousel number five."

After they had all gathered up their luggage, they made their way to Kevin's Mercedes Benz Sprinter and then piled in for the hour-and-a-half drive down to the Jersey Shore.

At around two o'clock, they got off the parkway at exit 98 and then turned onto Route 34 south toward Point Pleasant Beach. As they drove

112

through Point Pleasant, Liv pointed out some of her favorite spots—the original Jersey Mike's, Hoffman's ice cream, and the Brave New World Surf Shop. After crossing the railroad tracks, they entered Bay Head, a sleepy little shore town that rested between the Atlantic Ocean and the Barnegat Bay. Since 1879, the town had been a haven for boaters and beachgoers alike. The main street of Bay Head was lined with small shops and exceptional restaurants. And even though the town was less than one square mile, it boasted over 550 historical homes, most of which were built by Liv's great-grandfather way back in the 1920s. Liv had always been beyond grateful for every summer that she had lived in this magnificent little town. As a child, her summer days were spent at the Bay Head Yacht Club where she had enjoyed sailing, tennis, and, on Friday nights, dinner dances. Every August, she'd looked forward to the annual clambake on the beach. And on Sundays, after church service at All Saints, she couldn't wait to get home for a slice of crumb cake from Mueller's bakery. For Liv, Bay Head was not just a town, but a way of life that had now become embedded into her soul.

Turning down East Avenue, Liv pointed out the homes of her childhood friends and family to Beau. When they reached 406 East Avenue, Kevin pulled into her parent's gravel driveway. As soon as they all got out of the car, Liv could hear the familiar sound of the waves crashing onto the beach. She smiled as she took in a deep breath of the familiar Atlantic sea air that she loved so much.

Looking up at their shingle-style family home that was accented by white shutters, she noticed right away that the hydrangea and rose bushes were all in full bloom. The boys ran ahead and up the slate steps that led to the enormous wraparound porch, which was shaded by green- and white-striped awnings. As soon as the boys entered the house, they raced up the main staircase to choose from the eight bedrooms that the home had to offer.

Beau, Liv, and Rose walked through the family room and then out onto the lower deck, which had a large screened-in gazebo, gourmet outdoor kitchen, and oval-shaped swimming pool. Liv immediately spotted her parents on the upper deck.

"Love, this is some house," said Beau.

"I know. It's a little slice of heaven, isn't it?"

"I'd say."

Once they climbed the stairs to the upper deck, Liv could hardly believe her eyes.

"David! What on earth are you doing here?" she said as she hugged her parents and then David.

"Liv, my grandmother isn't doing very well," replied David.

"Oh, no, David," said Liv. "I'm so sorry to hear that."

"Thanks, Liv. And welcome home, Jersey girl."

"It feels great to be back. Oh, Mom and Dad, this is Beau Walker."

"Nice to meet both of you," said Beau. "And I must say, this is some home you have here," he added, as he took in the scenery. As far as the eye could see up and down the coast were wooden decks that were perched upon rolling, grass-covered dunes. Each deck was accented by an American flag that waved proudly in the crisp Atlantic breeze.

"Liv's great-grandfather certainly did have a talent for building beach houses," said Liv's father, Peter.

"That's for sure," said Beau.

Just then, the boys tore out of the house in their bathing trunks and waved as they raced down the dune and dove into the brisk Atlantic sea.

Liv's mother smiled. "It's so nice to have you all back here," she said.

"I think I'll go across the street and throw on my suit," said David.

"The ocean looks amazing," said Beau. "And I could sure go for an afternoon swim."

"I want to go swimming, too, Mommy!" exclaimed Rose.

Beau bent down and picked up Rose. "Liv, if you put her swimsuit on, I'd be happy to take her down for a swim."

"Okay, thanks, Beau." Liv, Beau, and Rose all headed back toward the house, then reappeared shortly with Rose dressed in her bathing suit. Liv and her mother stayed behind on the deck while everyone else went down for an afternoon swim.

"Look at all of them," Liv said, gazing out at the ocean and smiling.

"So, Olivia, please tell me. How are you really doing?" asked her mother.

"Well, Mother, it sure hasn't been easy, that's for sure," Liv replied.

"Still no word from him?"

"No, not really. My attorney told me he's been on some super yacht cruising around the French Riviera."

"Olivia, I just don't understand him. We all treated him like a part of this family for years. I mean, c'mon, how many summers did he spend sitting on this very deck?"

"I know, Mom, but it's like he's a completely different person now. And to be honest, I'm also starting to feel as though I never truly knew him."

"Well, you and I both know you're better off without him."

"Mom, I one hundred percent agree with you. But it's still not easy. Especially on the kids."

"Liv, believe me, my heart breaks for my grandchildren. But Olivia, please do tell me, what exactly is going on with you and Beau?"

Liv and her mom watched as Beau rode a wave to shore with Rose on his back.

"We're just good friends, Mom. That's all. Nothing more."

"Well, Liv, that's a shame. He's incredibly handsome. And it looks as though all of your children adore him."

"Mom, Don't get me wrong. He's definitely been a huge blessing, and I do truly value his friendship, but trust me, Mom, we're just friends."

"Well, not to worry, Olivia. There's always David. That man has been pining away for you for twenty-plus years now."

"Oh, Mother, that ship sailed many moons ago."

"My darling daughter, there's where you're wrong. Ships have a way of changing their course. And sometimes, they even find their way back to you. I think I'll invite him to our lobster dinner tomorrow night."

Liv knew there was no arguing with her mother, and besides, she did enjoy spending time with David.

Soon, the kids raced back up the dune, rinsed off at the outdoor shower, and jumped into the pool.

"What time is dinner, Mom?" asked Liv.

"Everything is being delivered at seven."

"Okay, I'll go set the table in the gazebo after I change and unpack."

Liv turned to go.

"Olivia," said her mom, "before you go inside, come here and give your mother a hug." Liv embraced her mother. "My darling daughter, please put all of your worries away. You're home now," Liv's mom whispered.

"Thanks, Mom. I'll try."

At seven o'clock, all eight of them gathered in the screened-in gazebo for some of Lenny's specialties—pizza, eggplant Parmesan, spaghetti and meatballs, chicken rigatoni, and tortilla Alfredo. They passed the food around the table as Liv's father opened up one wine bottle after another.

Liv gazed out at the ocean and then looked around the table. Beau was gently wiping spaghetti sauce off of Rose's face as her boys were fighting over the last slice of pizza. Liv's mother raised her wineglass.

"To family," she said. They all clinked glasses and echoed, "To family."

Thankfully, Olivia Whittaker had found her way back home and was once again in her parents' loving arms.

CHAPTER 19

Aunt Betty

When Liv returned from her beach walk the following morning, she found her mother and Rose sitting on the deck throwing a tennis ball for their beloved golden retriever, Sandy. Rose clapped with delight each time Sandy brought the ball back to her.

"So, Mom, what's the plan for today?" asked Liv.

"Well, I don't expect the men to be back from fishing until sometime after two o'clock," her mom replied.

"I really hope they have a good day out there," said Liv.

"I'm sure they're going to have a blast with cousin Roger. Aunt Betty told me they're going for fluke, and you know Roger won't be satisfied until the boat is filled with fish. In the meantime, I've invited Aunt Betty over for a girls' lunch and gossip session in the gazebo."

"Oh, Mom, that sounds perfect." Aunt Betty was by far Liv's favorite aunt. She was a real free spirit and always a ball of fun. In high school, whenever Liv was having boy troubles, she would go over to Aunt Betty's. Aunt Betty would greet her at the front door with a glass of wine and a hug. They would then order Chinese food and sort out Liv's love life over chicken lo mein and eggrolls. In Liv's mind, there was no one on the planet who was kinder or more loving than her Aunt Betty.

"Oh, but first, Margaret called when you were out on your walk."

"She did?" Margaret was a longtime neighborhood friend of Liv's.

"Yes, and she's invited Rose to join her and her four kids for a picnic and a day of crabbing over on the bay."

"Well, that was awfully nice of her. And I know Rose will love that."

"She'll be here in an hour to pick her up."

"Okay, Mom, I'll bring Rose into the house and get her ready. What time is Aunt Betty coming over?"

"Noon."

"Great. I can't wait to see her."

At twelve noon, on the dot, Aunt Betty walked down the boardwalk carrying a grocery bag, yelling, "Where's my Livvy?"

Liv threw open the screen door of the gazebo and shouted, "Here I am, Auntie!" She then ran down the boardwalk and took the grocery bag out of Aunt Betty's hands.

Once they were back in the gazebo, Aunt Betty said, "Now, come and give your old aunt a hug." Liv squeezed her as hard as she could. "Well, Liv, I know you've been through hell but I must say, you look fabulous."

"Thanks, Auntie."

Liv's mother opened the screen door of the gazebo and set down two bottles of champagne on the table as Liv placed the chicken salad sandwiches from the Normandy Market on a large serving platter.

"Auntie, I'm so glad you came over today, and you have no idea how much I've missed you."

"Oh, Livvy, I've missed you too," said Aunt Betty. "And doesn't the table look pretty?"

"Liv did it, of course," said Liv's mom. "She's been out front cutting roses and hydrangeas every morning since she got here."

Aunt Betty reached over and squeezed Liv's hand and then took a sip of champagne. "Gosh, that tastes good. So tell me Livvy, how is my girl?" Aunt Betty had two sons, Roger and Russell, so she had always thought of Liv as more of a daughter than a niece.

"Well, Auntie, it's been rough," Liv replied.

"I can't even imagine," Aunt Betty said, nodding. "How are the kids?"

"They're doing okay. The boys never even mention Kurt."

"Liv, have you heard from him?"

"Not really, just a few text messages here and there. My attorney told me that he's on some super yacht in the French Riviera."

Aunt Betty took a big sip of her champagne and said, "He's a real piece of work, isn't he? So, Liv, what the hell do you think happened? I mean, you two were like Barbie and Ken, the perfect couple, the perfect family, the perfect house."

"Well, Auntie, as you know, nothing is ever perfect."

"And what about all of us? That man never even knew his own father and, after that outrageous stunt his mother pulled at your wedding, sleeping with his best man, he never spoke to her again. C'mon, Liv, let's face it, we've all been the only family that he has had for the last twenty years. Not to mention how my husband and sons have always included him on their annual hunting trips. I'm telling you, Olivia, the whole thing makes me sick to my stomach."

"I know Auntie, but at this point, I'm just trying to take it one day at a time, and move on the best I can."

"Well, kid, I give you a lot of credit, and I completely agree with you. You need to stay focused on the children and move on with your life. So, Livvy, what's this I heard about you bringing someone home with you? I want to hear all about him."

"Oh, Auntie, I think you might have the wrong idea about Beau."

"His name is Beau? Wow, that's super sexy!"

Oh, brother, thought Liv. "So here's the thing, Auntie. He's actually turning out to be a really dear friend and I'm very grateful to have him in my life."

"So what's the problem? He sounds perfect."

"I just think we're better off as friends, if you know what I mean."

"Actually, I don't," said Aunt Betty.

"Well," said Liv's mom, "I must say he's quite charming and he's fantastic with the kids."

"How old is he?" asked Aunt Betty. "Does he have kids? Has he ever been married? I want the scoop."

"So, I thought he was thirty-three," Liv replied, "but I got a glimpse of his driver's license at the airport and he's actually thirty-six. And, no, he's never been married and he doesn't have kids."

"Livvy, I'd be rethinking this whole *just friends* idea if I were you. Take your old aunt's advice and take this handsome fella out for a test drive, if you know what I mean," Auntie said as she took another sip of her champagne and winked at Liv.

"Auntie!"

"Don't worry, Betty," said Liv's mom, "I've invited David for dinner tonight. That fire is still burning between him and Liv. Plus, a little friendly competition between men is always a good thing."

"Mom, Auntie, you're both way too much."

Aunt Betty and Liv's mom both laughed.

"But wait a minute," said Aunt Betty. "I heard another one is coming to stay for the weekend. What's *his* name?"

"Chase Montgomery," said Liv. "So when Austin was growing up, Chase was like an older brother to him, and now we've become really great friends."

"Well, Livvy, I must say, it seems to me like you're doing just fine."

"Auntie, I just want my divorce to be finalized," said Liv, "so we can all begin to heal and move on. But I'll tell you one thing, I can never imagine walking down that aisle again. That's for damn sure."

"Livvy, take it from your old but wise aunt. You'll walk down that aisle again someday. You're still young, Olivia, and believe me, whether you like it or not, when you least expect it, love will find you again. That much I can promise you."

Liv smiled and took a sip of her champagne and thought, *I think it already has.*

CHAPTER 20

The Lobster Dinner

As predicted, the men returned with a boatload of fish, which Cousin Roger graciously cleaned and filleted. Liv's mother was thrilled to add fluke francaise to her lobster dinner menu.

Meanwhile, Liv made sure the dinner table was set perfectly for their annual lobster feast. Upon a red-and-white-checkered tablecloth, she set her great-grandmother's Spode Trade Winds dinner plates, sterling silver flatware, and Waterford Clarendon Ruby wine goblets. In front of each place setting was a silver lobster claw cracker and matching seafood fork that had been brought over from Ireland by her great-great-grandparents. Liv filled three Waterford Crimson vases with red and pink roses from her mother's garden. Last but not least, she placed three beeswax candles into hurricane lanterns.

As Liv stepped back to admire her work, her mother called in from the kitchen, "Liv, please come and help me bring up the groceries from my car."

"Mom, do you think you got enough food?" laughed Liv when she saw her mother's trunk.

"That's enough, Olivia," said her mom. "Where is everyone, anyways?"

"The guys are all body surfing with Dad, and Rose is taking a nap after her long day of crabbing out on the bay."

"Okay, well let's get this all up to the kitchen so I can get organized."

After making what felt to be endless trips back and forth from her mother's car, all of the food was finally arranged in the kitchen.

"So, Mom, what exactly are you serving tonight for dinner?" asked Liv.

"Steamers, of course, followed by Spikes Manhattan clam chowder. I bought nine three-pound lobsters from the Point Lobster Company that I'm going to bake and stuff." Liv knew that to steam a lobster in the Whittaker household was a sin. Baked and stuffed was the only way to go. "I went down to Big Ed's Produce Stand," her mother continued, "and picked up sweet corn, green beans, and, of course, Jersey tomatoes. I'm also going to make a batch of my scalloped potatoes. And last but not least, we're having Charlie's cheesecake for dessert."

"Wow, Mom, this is going to be some dinner. What can I do to help?"

"For starters, you can take the corn out to the deck and husk it, and then snap off the ends of the green beans."

"Okay, Mom, you got it."

After hours of cooking, the lobsters were in the oven and the steamers were on the stove.

"What time do you want us all at the table, Mom?" asked Liv.

"Tell everyone that dinner will be served in thirty minutes."

Liv opened the front door and started to walk out to the deck to give everyone a dinner update when she heard, "Hi, Liv, am I too early?" It was David, carrying a huge bouquet of flowers and wearing a blue and pink Madras shirt, navy shorts, and Docksider loafers.

"Oh no, David, you're not too early at all."

"Good," he said as he handed her the flowers. In the bouquet were ivory and pale pink roses, along with pink peonies and—Liv's favorite flower—hydrangeas.

"You remembered!" she said.

"Of course I did," said David. "I remember every moment we've ever spent together."

Just then, William called down from the upper deck. "Mom, is dinner almost ready? We're all starving."

"Yes, William, don't worry. We're all going to sit down very soon." Then she turned back to David. "Thank you. These are gorgeous. Why don't you go up to the deck, and I'll bring you out a cocktail. Johnny Black on the rocks, right?"

"That's it."

"Well, I guess I remember some things about you too," she said, smiling. Liv then went inside and carefully arranged the flowers in a crystal vase.

"Olivia," her mother said to her when she saw the flowers, "when are you ever going to listen to your mother? That man is still in love with you."

Liv stared out the kitchen window remembering the day when David had proposed to her on the upper deck all those years ago.

"Tell me, Olivia," her mother said, "how do you really feel about him?"

"I'm not sure, Mom. When I look at him, I remember the great love we once had. But that was a very long time ago."

"Well, I think you owe it to yourself to have an honest conversation with him about everything that has happened."

"I know, Mom. You're right."

"Okay, well please put those beautiful flowers on the table and then tell everyone that dinner is officially ready."

At seven o'clock, the family gathered around the table to enjoy their very traditional Jersey Shore lobster dinner.

"Mrs. Whittaker," said Beau, "you have truly outdone yourself. And I'm embarrassed to say this, but I've never had steamers before. But now I can assure you that I'm a fan for life."

"Beau, I'm so glad you like them," said Liv's mom. "And they're so much sweeter than steamed clams."

"Nana, everything is terrific," said William.

"Can I have another ear of corn?" asked Jeffrey.

"And I'll have another scoop of your world-famous scalloped pota-toes, please," said David.

"The lobster is wonderful, Mom," said Liv.

"Baked and stuffed—it's the only way to go," said Liv's mom.

Liv's father raised his wineglass. "Cheers to my beautiful family, to new and old friends, and to summers at the Jersey Shore."

"Cheers!" they all replied and clinked glasses.

After enjoying their lobster feast, everyone pitched in to clean up. When the last dish was placed in the dishwasher, William said, "Mom, we're all going to head over to the Parker House now, if that's okay."

"That's fine, William," said Liv. "Just please call Briggs taxi service. I know how wild the Parker House can get in the summertime, and I don't want any of you drinking and driving."

"Okay, Mom, no worries," said William. "Beau, do you want to come?"

"Beau, You should definitely go," said Liv. "The Parker House is a Jersey Shore institution. It's a very large Victorian beach home that was built in the 1900s. It has a huge wraparound front porch, indoor restau-rant, and the downstairs is a dance club. Trust me, you'll love it."

"Okay, I'm game," said Beau. "And thanks again for dinner, Mrs. Whittaker."

"Anytime, Beau. Now please promise to take good care of my grand
sons tonight."

"Not to worry, Mrs. Whittaker. I promise to keep an eye on them,"
said Beau, and with that, the guys were off.

"Mom," said Liv, "It looks as though Rose has fallen asleep on the
living room sofa. I better get her up to bed."

"Olivia, your father and I can put Rose to bed. But I believe there's
some unfinished business waiting for you outside."

"Wait, is David still here?"

Liv's mom nodded.

"Okay," said Liv. "I guess it's now or never." She kissed Rose on the
cheek and then went outside, slowly walking down the boardwalk and
up the stairs to the upper deck where David was sitting.

"So, where is everyone?" he asked.

"The guys all took off to the Parker House," Liv replied.

"Classic."

"And my parents are putting Rose to bed. Can I get you anything else?"

"Oh, no, thanks. I'm stuffed. I really shouldn't have had that second
piece of cheesecake, but I just couldn't resist."

"I know. It really is to die for."

"So, would you like to take a walk on the beach?" asked David.

"Sure," Liv replied nervously.

Liv had to admit to herself that she'd been thinking about this moment
for over twenty years. As they walked over the dune, David slid his hand
into hers. "Do you want to go up on the lifeguard stand?" he asked.

Liv thought back and remembered how David had first kissed her
on the lifeguard stand all those years ago. "Okay."

David took her hand and helped her climb up. They sat side by
side and stared out at the ocean. Liv sighed and said, "Okay, David. So
there are a few things that I really need to say to you."

"Okay."

The words didn't come easily at first. What do you say to the man whom you thought you were going to spend the rest of your life with, but who instead ended up going to prison for selling cocaine? Finally, Liv blurted out, "How could you have done this to me?! And I'm not just talking about your prison sentence. I'm talking about how I wrote to you every week for a year with no response! David, I wanted nothing more than to hear from you. I would have stood by you, but, no, not a word for four years! So I ended up marrying Kurt, thank you very much. But if only you had just answered *one* of my letters or would have allowed me to visit you, my life—no, *our lives*—would be completely different. We would be sitting here on this lifeguard stand married! We would have watched our children run and play on this very beach. But no, your ego and pride ruined everything. Everything!" Liv was crying now.

David gently reached up and wiped away her tears. "Liv, it's not what you think. I was just trying to protect you. I've known you and your family my entire life. And I didn't want you to come to the prison, Liv. I couldn't ask that of you. My prison sentence was my mistake, not yours. I wanted to serve my time like a man and not drag you into my mess."

"David, that's where you're wrong. I had agreed to be your wife. We should have gone through that together. But no, David, you left me." Liv began to sob uncontrollably.

David put his arm around her and pulled her close to him. "Liv, I'm so sorry. You have to know that. You also have to know that I'm still in love with you."

"I know you are," said Liv. "And I'm still in love with you, but every time I look at you, I see the way things could have been for both of us and it breaks my heart."

David held Liv tightly as she continued to sob, twenty plus years of pent-up emotions spilling out of her. Finally, she pulled herself together and stared into David's eyes. He leaned over and kissed her. She kissed him back.

Liv's mother was right. The spark between the two of them had never died. David started kissing Liv's neck as his hand slowly moved up her thigh and between her legs. He pushed her panties to the side and slid his finger inside of her. She reached down and touched him. She started to unzip his pants and then stopped herself.

"I'm sorry, David," she said. "I just can't do this."

"Liv, please let me make love to you. I'm begging you."

"No, David, you don't understand," said Liv.

"Understand what, Liv?"

"David, there's someone else." And with that, she jumped off the lifeguard stand and ran up the dune as fast as she could.

CHAPTER 21

"May the Best Man Win!"

Liv tossed and turned all night reliving the events from the night before. Finally, at 5:45 a.m., she threw on her workout clothes and decided to go for a long walk on the beach.

As she walked along the shoreline, the sand was cool under her feet. She glanced up towards the west. The moon was still shining with a few twinkling stars remaining, and to the east, the first colors of dawn were coming out over the horizon. The cold Atlantic Ocean washed over her toes as she breathed in the briny sea air.

After about forty-five minutes into her walk, she stopped to watch the sun rise majestically over the ocean. The sun was a fiery pink ball that morning. She took out her cell phone to capture the moment. She then slid her phone back into her pocket and turned around to head back to her parents' house. A beach walk might not be able to fix everything, but for Liv, it was always a good start.

When her parents' house came into view, she noticed a figure standing with his arms crossed at the shoreline and she knew immediately that it was David. He was sliding his right foot back and forth across the sand, staring out at the horizon. He turned and spotted her and then slowly began to walk towards her. When he finally reached Liv, he stopped and crossed his arms once again.

"How did you sleep last night?" he asked.

"I didn't. What about you?"

"Not a wink, Liv. I figured I'd find you down here. You always go for a beach walk whenever you're upset."

"I guess you really do know me, David."

"Liv, I know your heart inside and out."

"I know you do. And I know yours. That's why this is so very difficult. And on top of everything else, our families have been friends for over fifty years."

"Who is it?" David asked.

"What?"

"Who's the guy?"

Liv looked down at the sand and quietly said, "It's Chase."

"Chase? The young guy I met at your golf event?"

"Yes, David, and by the way, he's not that young."

"What, is he like twelve or something?"

"David, that's not fair."

"No, seriously, how old is he?"

"He's thirty-one."

"Olivia, you're in love with a thirty-one year old? Oh my God, Liv, have you lost your mind?"

"David, you're just jealous."

"Well, hell yeah, I am, but I'm also being honest. Liv, He's way too young for you. And don't get me wrong. I'm sure you'll have fun with him for a while, but I'm telling you, it will never last. Jesus, Liv, does your family know?"

"No. And I don't want them to find out."

"Why not? If he's the man of your dreams, don't you want the whole world to know?"

"Look, David, this is a very complicated situation that I'm in. Chase and I have only just started to date, not to mention the fact that I'm not even divorced yet. And yes, I'm very nervous to tell my family."

"Well, is he good to you?"

"Yes, David. He's been so incredibly sweet, kind, and loving with me."

"Well, he better be, or he'll have me to answer to."

Liv smiled. "Look, David, after everything that I've been through lately, I've come to realize that as carefully as you think you can plan out your life, you can never know what the future might hold. David, I really thought I was going to be married to Kurt forever and now, look. I'm getting divorced and I'm a single mother to four kids. David, I guess what I'm trying to say is, you're right. I don't know what's going to happen with me and Chase, but I need to give us a chance, and as far as you and me goes, I do know that I will always love you, David. And I've also spent too many years without you in my life. The fact of the matter is, I've missed you, David, and, like I said, I have no idea what my future holds, but I do know this: I really want you to be a part of it." Liv looked up at him with tears in her eyes. He hugged her.

"Don't worry, Liv," he said, "I'm not going anywhere. I'll always be here for you no matter what. I hope you know that."

"I do."

"Well, then. As they say, 'may the best man win,'" he stated as he gave her another big hug.

CHAPTER 22

A Day on the Boardwalk

After Liv finished her conversation with David on the beach, she walked up the dune to find her mother sitting on the deck enjoying her morning coffee and throwing the ball for Sandy.

"Seeing you two standing on the water's edge was like stepping back in time," her mother said as Liv took a seat on the deck.

"Mom, you don't know the half of it."

"So, Liv, what happened last night?" Liv filled her mother in on her conversation with David.

"Olivia, are you sure you don't want to give him another chance?"

"Mom, I'm not sure of anything right now. I just want to focus on my kids and my upcoming divorce. And after that, who knows?"

Just then, Beau appeared on the walkway carrying a surfboard.

"Good morning, Beau," said Liv. "You're up early."

"Well, Liv, I didn't stay out very late last night," said Beau. "I ended up taking a cab back here around midnight. That crowd over at the Parker House was way too young for my taste."

Liv smiled as she thought back to the age on Beau's driver's license: thirty-six.

"Besides," Beau continued, "aren't we going to take Rose to the boardwalk today? I promised to win her a teddy bear, remember?"

"Yep, that's the plan."

"Well, Love, I'm all yours. What time should I be ready?"

"I thought we'd leave around noon, if that's okay."

"Sounds perfect. I'm going to go catch some waves, but don't worry. I'll be ready to leave at noon." And with that, Beau ran down the dune and into the surf.

"I don't know, Liv," said Liv's mother.

"You don't know what, Mom?"

"I'm beginning to think that Beau Walker is falling in love with you."

Liv could feel herself begin to blush. "Mom, we're just good friends and nothing more." She stood up and started walking towards the house.

"The best relationships are based on friendship, you know," her mother called out after her.

Liv shook her head as she opened the front door.

At twelve noon, Beau, Liv, and Rose walked into the Wharfside Restaurant, which had been serving locals since 1963. The Wharfside was a large establishment on the water with a huge outdoor deck and dramatic views of the Manasquan Inlet and Barnegat Bay.

The hostess sat them at a wooden booth that overlooked the water. Rose was mesmerized by the boats weaving in and out of the inlet. Fishing boats went by with their nets full of their morning catch, while seagulls flew close behind, scooping up the discarded bait. Over on the sandbar, dogs ran across the sand, catching Frisbees that were being tossed into the air.

When the waitress came by their booth to take their order, Liv said, "We're both going to share the steamers and the fried clams, and my daughter will have the kids' chicken fingers and fries, please."

"Would you also like me to bring over the salad cart, our homemade hushpuppies, and coleslaw?" asked the waitress.

"Yes, yes, and yes," Beau replied with a big grin.

"We'll also have two glasses of Kendall Jackson Chardonnay, please," said Liv, "and my daughter will have a Sprite."

"You got it. I'll be right back with your drinks and the salad cart."

Before long, they were all enjoying their lunches. The waitress soon returned to the table and said, "I brought this bag of dried corn over for your daughter in case she wanted to go and feed the ducks."

"Yes, Mom, please?" asked Rose.

"Okay, Rose," said Liv. "Go sit on that bench over there but don't go any farther." Rose took the corn and ran off from the table.

"Well, Love," said Beau. "I must say, I'm definitely turning into a big fan of the Jersey Shore."

"Good," said Liv. "And don't you just love my hometown?"

"I have to tell you, Love, it's amazing. And so are your parents."

"Well, you've certainly made a big impression on both of them. And I'm pretty sure my mother's hoping we get married or something."

"What?!"

"Oh, never mind. My mother can just be a little overbearing at times. But, actually, Beau, I am a little curious about something."

"What is it, Love?"

"Have you ever been in love? You know, the crazy kind of love that just takes over your whole life?"

Beau took a big sip of his wine. "Once," he said. "But it was a very long time ago. She lived in New York and she had a daughter. The distance and the timing was all wrong. So, in the end, it just didn't work out."

"There hasn't been anyone else?"

"Nope."

"Well, I had a very interesting evening with David last night."

"Oh, yeah? What happened?"

Liv filled him in on the details of the night before and Beau said, "Well, Love, if you want my opinion, I think David is a great guy. Much better than that loser Chase."

"Beau, why do you dislike Chase so much?"

"He just has this air about him. Like he's better than everyone else. Plus, I definitely don't trust him."

Rose came running back to the table. "Can we go to the boardwalk now?" she asked. "Beau promised to win me a huge teddy bear."

"Yes I did," said Beau. "And I always keep my promises."

Once they arrived at the Point Pleasant Beach boardwalk, their first stop was to Jenkinson's Aquarium. Rose pressed her hands up to the glass as the penguins went waddling by. Beau put Rose on his shoulders so she could get a better view of the great white sharks and the giant stingrays swimming by. Upstairs, Beau helped Rose with the touch tank. He carefully picked up a starfish and gently placed it in her hand. Next, it was on to watch the seals. Rose laughed with delight watching the seals frolic and play.

After the aquarium, it was off to try to win Rose's teddy bear at the basketball hoop booth. Beau needed to sink ten basketballs in two minutes and on his first try, he did just that. Rose squealed as Beau handed her a giant panda bear.

"Thank you, Beau!" Rose said jumping up and down.

"Let's go on some rides now," Liv offered.

"Liv, first, I say we get a slice of pizza," said Beau.

"Beau, we just ate!"

"I know, but your father told me that I had to try a slice of board-walk pizza. And he also told me I needed to have a hot waffle ice cream sandwich."

"Oh, brother," said Liv. "Okay, if that's what my father said. I know just the spot." Liv walked them over to Marteli's and ordered two slices of pizza, a waffle ice cream sandwich, and a bag of zeppoles. As they continued to stroll down the boardwalk, they passed by the arcades, funhouse, gift shops, and games of chance.

"Let's take a quick ride on the boardwalk train," Liv suggested.

Beau, Liv, and Rose climbed aboard the train that circled around the section of children's rides and then traveled along the ocean catching the cool afternoon sea breeze. After the train ride, Beau turned to Rose and asked, "So, Rose, which rides would you like to go on?"

"All of them!" Rose beamed.

"Okay. Then all of them it is." Beau took Rose on the tilt-a-whirl, motorcycles, fire engines, helicopters, rollercoaster, bumper cars, and the Ferris wheel. The last ride of the day was the carousel. Liv, Beau, and Rose rode up and down on their painted horses as carousel music filled the air. Liv looked over at Rose who was grinning from ear to ear.

As they walked back to the car, Beau once again picked up Rose and placed her on his shoulders. He then reached over and took Liv's hand. Liv smiled up at him and thought to herself, on this summer afternoon in August, she was secretly hoping he would never let go.

CHAPTER 23

The Odd Man Out

When Liv entered the kitchen on Friday morning, she found her mother cooking up a huge breakfast buffet for the guys who were getting ready to head out for their day of golf at the Baltusrol Country Club.

"Wow, Mom, this is quite a feast," Liv said as she glanced over at the platters of French toast, scrambled eggs, and bacon.

David walked into the kitchen carrying his golf clubs. *What on earth is he doing here?* Liv thought.

"David, come grab a plate and help yourself to some breakfast," said Liv's mother.

"Good morning," David said to Liv as he reached for a plate.

"David, I didn't realize you were playing today," said Liv.

David took a bite of bacon and replied, "Well, Liv, your mom called me early this morning and asked if I could fill in for your father."

"Yes, Liv," said Liv's mom, "your father had an emergency come up at work, so I asked David to take his place."

"Oh, I see," said Liv.

"What are the teams again?" asked Beau.

Austin replied, "It's going to be you and William, me and Jeffrey, Brett and Uncle Rollins, and David is going to be playing with Chase."

"Sounds like a great day of golf to me," David said as he winked at Liv.

"David, can I speak to you in the living room for a moment?" Liv asked.

"Sure," replied David as he grabbed his breakfast plate and a glass of orange juice.

Once in the living room, Liv turned to David and said, "Listen, David, I don't know how you managed to get yourself invited on this golf outing—"

"Liv, your mother invited me. That's how, and why are you so angry?"

"Because, I just don't want you upsetting Chase is all."

"And how would I do that exactly? Look, Liv, I didn't even know I was going to be playing with him. So you can thank your son for that, but I will tell you this—I'm definitely going to take this opportunity to get to know him better."

"Well, David, that's what I'm afraid of."

"Listen, Liv, I've known you my entire life, and I'm always going to protect you until the day I die."

"David, that's very sweet, but I really don't need protecting."

"Liv, what's that old saying? *Love is blind.* And c'mon, let's face it, dopamine is a very powerful drug that can certainly cloud anyone's better judgment."

"David, just so we're clear, you are the last person I would ever take relationship advice from. Especially after everything you've put me through."

"Look, Liv, I'm sorry you're upset, but you have my word that everything is going to be fine today."

"Promise?"

"Yes, Liv, I promise."

Liv's mother called out from the kitchen, "Kevin is waiting for all of you in the driveway. So you need to hurry up and finish your breakfast."

David kissed Liv on the cheek. "See you tonight at dinner. And Liv, please stop worrying."

After an hour and twenty-minute drive, Kevin pulled up to the historic Baltusrol Golf Club, site of seven US Men's Opens, four US Men's Amateurs, two US Women's Opens, two US Women's Amateurs, and two PGA Championships.

The group walked into the stone clubhouse, which was built in 1895. The decor was rich fabrics, dark woods, and red leather club seats. Liv's cousin Brett and her Uncle Rollins were both waiting in the lobby to greet them.

"Welcome to Baltusrol, gentlemen," said Brett.

William introduced Beau to Brett and Uncle Rollins.

"I believe we're still waiting for one more?" asked Brett.

"Yes," replied Austin. "My buddy, Chase, is coming in from the city."

"Well, why don't we head over to the men's grille," suggested Brett, "and order a quick bite before hitting the course?"

As the group sat down to dine on club sandwiches, BLTs, and ham and Swiss on rye, in walked Chase. Austin introduced him to Brett and Uncle Rollins, and then they all caught up over lunch.

Afterwards, everyone went downstairs to the well-appointed men's locker room to change, and soon they were all out on the course.

"Just remember, gentlemen," said Uncle Rollins, as they loaded up the golf carts, "$400 is on the line today and, of course, bragging rights." And with that, the game got underway.

At hole nine, David pulled out two Romeo y Julieta cigars.

"Care for one?" he asked Chase.

"Thanks," Chase replied.

"So, how was the city?"

"Well, to be honest with you, I'm not much of a city guy, but the conference was a success overall."

"And what do you do again?"

"Oh, I'm a complex manager at Morgan Stanley."

"Nice. Do you like it?"

Chase put his ball on the tee and swung hard. "I do. The hours are long and I do travel quite a bit, but the money's good. And I'm very grateful to be back down at their Palm Beach office."

"So, I heard you were the guy who first taught Austin how to play golf," said David before swinging off the tee.

"I did, but to tell you the truth, Austin was sinking putts all on his own at the age of three. The kid's a natural."

"He sure is." The two jumped into the cart and drove down the fairway. "Speaking of kids," said David, "I also heard you're quite good with Rose."

"Well, David, as you know, Rose is a special little girl, and her smile truly does light up any room."

"Just like her mother's," David said. "Hey, Chase, did you know I was engaged to Liv, many moons ago?"

"I did."

They got off the cart, each grabbing a five-iron.

"You know, Chase, it's funny how you really never do get over your first love," said David. "Speaking of love, I imagine you must have a swarm of girls trying to get you down the aisle."

141

Chase laughed as he chipped his ball onto the green. "David, I think you're exaggerating just a bit. And to tell you the truth, with my busy work schedule, I don't really have time for a love life right now."

"Well, surely, you must want to get married and have children someday." Then David chipped onto the green.

"Perhaps one day. But right now, I'm just focusing on my career. Besides, look at you. You've never been married, no kids, and you seem like a pretty happy guy to me."

"Buddy, don't let outward appearances fool you," said David, sinking his putt. "I would give anything to change my past and have the woman of my dreams by my side. But God does have a funny way of working things out for us, and luckily, Liv is once again back in my life." David watched Chase sink his putt into the hole and then gave him a piercing look before continuing. "And I have absolutely no intention of ever letting her go again."

After being out on the course for over four hours, the guys all met back at the men's grille for a round of Dark and Stormies. Austin tallied up the scores and announced, "So it would appear that David and Chase have won today's round."

"Well done, gentlemen," said Uncle Rollins as he raised his glass.

David raised his glass in return and said, "To a great day of golf with a great group of men." They all clinked their glasses, and then they headed down to the locker room to shower and change before driving back to the shore.

By 7:30, they were walking through the doors of the Off Shore Restaurant. The hostess escorted them to the fireplace room where Liv, Rose, and her parents were already seated.

Liv jumped up and gave Chase a big hug. "Welcome to the Jersey Shore!" she said. "Chase, these are my parents, Victoria and Peter."

Liv's father stood up and shook Chase's hand and said, "Glad you could come down for the weekend."

"Yes, we're delighted you could join us," Victoria added.

"How was golf today?" asked Peter. "I'm sorry I couldn't make it."

"David and Chase were the big winners today," announced Beau. "They beat us all by a landslide."

"Excellent," replied Peter.

"I must say, I think Baltusrol is one of the most beautiful and challenging courses that I've ever played on," said David.

"Well, David," said Peter, "I've known you since the day you were born, and you've never been afraid of a challenge."

"That's for damn sure, Peter, and I'm still not," said David as he looked across the table at Liv.

Liv could feel herself begin to blush. Fortunately, the waitress appeared just then, carrying three bar pies, three orders of clams casino, and three orders of calamari.

Liv leaned over and whispered to Chase, "Did you have fun today?"

"Liv, We'll talk about what happened today later."

Suddenly, Liv felt very nervous.

Over dinner, the group recapped the week's events.

"Beau, you definitely caught the most fish the other day out on Roger's boat," said William.

"What can I say?" said Beau. "I'm a natural-born fisherman."

"Beau, I'm grateful that you did so well out there," said Victoria. "And thanks to you, I was able to add flounder to our lobster dinner menu."

"Victoria," said David, "that dinner you made for us was excellent. Thanks again for having me."

"Yes," said Beau. "It was my first time having steamers and now I'm a huge fan. Chase, have you ever had steamers before?"

"No, I can't say that I have," Chase replied.

"Well, buddy, you missed out. And Liv took me to the prettiest spot on the water the other day for lunch. Liv, what was the name of that restaurant again?"

"The Wharfside," Liv quietly replied.

Then Rose exclaimed, "Beau won me the biggest panda bear in the whole wide world at the boardwalk!"

"Yes, I must say, this has been some week," said Beau. "Sorry you missed so much of it, Chase."

"Well, Beau, not all of us have a flexible work schedule like you," replied Chase. Chase felt a shift in the group. Suddenly, he was the outsider. And somehow over the course of the week, the guys had all bonded. Even David and Beau seemed to be best buddies. Chase excused himself to go to the restroom. Moments later, Liv received a text: *Liv, we really need to talk!*

At the table, Liv's phone buzzed. She read the text. *This can't be good*, she thought.

After dinner, everyone gathered on the restaurant's front porch to take some group photos. Liv pulled Chase aside. "Is everything okay?" she asked.

"No, Liv," Chase replied. "It's definitely not."

"Come on, Liv," called Peter as the valets pulled up the cars.

"Coming, Dad." She turned and walked quickly across the parking lot.

Once they were all back at the house, the guys decided to have bourbon and cigars out on the deck. Liv's mom put Rose to bed as Liv gave Chase a tour of the house.

"And this is my room," Liv said as she opened the door to her bedroom. "It hasn't changed one bit since my childhood."

"Well, Liv, speaking of your childhood, David made it quite clear to me today that he's still in love with you."

"Is that why you're so mad? Chase, you have no reason to be jealous of him. And besides, all of that happened a million years ago."

"Listen, Liv, I'm pretty sure he still wants you to be his wife. And when did he and Beau become such good friends?"

"Look, Chase, I'm sorry you're upset."

"Well, you'd be upset too if you were me. And what's this about you and Beau having a romantic lunch on the water?"

"Chase, I'm telling you, you're making way too much out of all of this."

"Well, Liv, maybe me coming down here wasn't such a good idea after all."

Liv took Chase's hand and said, "Chase, Please don't say that. I'm so happy that you're here. And you have no idea how much I've missed you." She put her arms around him and kissed his neck.

"Liv, it's just hard, and also, I really wish we could tell everyone how we feel about each other."

Just then, Austin came into the room and Liv immediately stepped back away from Chase.

"Hey, man, I've been looking everywhere for you. Don't you want to come out to the deck and have a cocktail and a cigar with us?"

"Sure, Austin," Chase replied. "Your mom was just giving me a tour of the house."

"Austin, let me show Chase to his room," said Liv, "and then we'll both be out."

"Okay, Mom," said Austin.

"So, where is my room anyway?" asked Chase as he picked up his suitcase.

"Well, Chase, unfortunately, I had to put you in with Rose because all the other bedrooms are already taken."

"Oh, that's fine," said Chase. "At least *she* likes me. Well, she did until Beau won her 'the biggest panda bear in the whole wide world,'" he added, in a teasing voice as he rolled his eyes.

"Well, *I* like you," Liv said, and then she kissed him. "It's *you* Chase, and only you. You know that right?"

Chase nodded. "Promise?"

"Promise," Liv said as she took him by the hand and led him down the hallway to Rose's room.

CHAPTER 24

The Heart Wants What the Heart Wants

The next morning, the house was filled with a bustle of activity. Soiree Caterers had arrived and were setting up for the Gallagher family brunch. When Liv passed by the dining room table, she noticed a bagel platter as well as an assortment of cream cheese, a fruit platter, donuts, crumb cake, and Danishes, all from Mueller's bakery.

Meanwhile, Liv's mother was busy in the kitchen directing the catering staff.

"If you could please set up the omelet, waffle, and pancake stations in the living room, that would be great," she said.

The bartender asked, "Mrs. Gallagher, where do you want the Mimosa station and Bloody Mary bar set up?"

"Oh, that's going to go outside next to the pool," she replied.

"Let's go," the bartender said as two staff members followed behind him wheeling out ten cases of Veuve Clicquot.

"Mom, do you think that maybe you've gone just a tad bit overboard?" Liv asked when she entered the kitchen.

"Nonsense, Olivia. This is your welcome home party and I want everything to be perfect."

Just then Beau walked into the kitchen. "Some guys are at the front door," he said. "They want to know where the tent should go."

"Tent?" said Liv. "Mother, you got a tent?"

"Of course I did. There's a twenty percent chance of rain today, so, as they say, better to be safe than sorry."

"Good morning, everyone," said Liv's father as he walked into the kitchen carrying two grocery bags. He placed the bags on the kitchen counter and began pulling out boxes of pork roll, Thumann's hotdogs, and burgers.

"Peter, what on earth are you doing?" asked Liv's mother.

"Listen, Victoria, Not everyone likes all this fancy stuff that you're serving here today so I've decided to grill up some Jersey Shore staples. Hey, Beau, I bet you never had a Thumann's hotdog or a pork roll sandwich before, am I right?"

"No, sir," replied Beau.

"Well, you can't come to the Jersey Shore without having a proper barbecue. Now, if you'll excuse me, I'm going to go and fire up the grill." And with that, he walked out the back door.

"Olivia, I'm telling you," said Liv's mother, "sometimes I could just strangle that man."

"Oh, Mom, don't worry. Today is going to be great. So what time does everyone arrive?"

"Around noon."

"Do you need me to do anything?"

"No, darling, I got this."

"Okay, Mom. Well, in that case, I guess I'll go upstairs to change and get Rose dressed."

At noon sharp, Liv and Rose were out on the upper deck dressed in their matching Lilly Pulitzer shifts. Her family had begun to arrive, and Liv had to admit that her mother had done a beautiful job with the brunch. Chase walked out the front door wearing a pale blue Vineyard Vines polo shirt and navy shorts.

"Hey, handsome. You look very nice," said Liv.

"Well, Liv, I'm hoping to make a good impression on your family today," Chase said.

"Chase, Not to worry. I'm sure they're all going to love you."

"Hey, what's your dad doing over at the grill?"

"Oh, he's attempting to drive my mother crazy," Liv said as she rolled her eyes. "He thought it would be nice to grill up some Jersey Shore favorites for the family."

"Well, I think I'll go make a Bloody Mary and give him a hand."

"Livvy?"

Liv turned around and saw her Aunt Betty walking down the boardwalk. "Chase," Liv said, "before you head over to the grill, come and meet my aunt." Liv and Chase walked over to Aunt Betty and Liv did the introductions. "Auntie, this is Chase Montgomery."

"Nice to meet you, young man," said Aunt Betty. "Liv has told me so many wonderful things about you."

"Well," said Chase, "between you and me, Auntie, Liv does have a tendency to over-exaggerate sometimes." They all laughed. "Auntie, I was just going to head over to the Bloody Mary bar. Would you like to join me?"

"Of course I would," Aunt Betty replied. "With this many relatives around, I could definitely use a good stiff drink."

Auntie and Chase wandered over to the Bloody Mary bar while Liv caught up with the rest of the family. Then she went into the house and made a plate for Rose and one for herself. After she got Rose settled at a picnic table with her cousins, she headed back to the upper deck.

"Wow, Mom, this is quite a turnout," she said.

"Yes, it looks as though all of the Gallaghers are here and accounted for."

"And Mom, Thanks again for doing all of this. It really is so nice to see everyone again."

"Well, it's great to have you home, darling. Wait—did you see that?"

"See what, Mom?"

"Your father is feeding Sandy hotdogs!"

And with that, Liv's mom rushed off the deck.

"Livvy," said Aunt Betty, "come sit here. I've saved a seat for you."

Liv took a seat next to her aunt.

"Livvy, This is some spread your mother has for all of us today," said Auntie.

"I know. And between you and me, I think she went a little overboard. But it is nice to have the family all together again. So how's the Bloody Mary, Auntie?"

"Divine. I told Chase to make it hot and spicy, just like I like my men."

"Auntie, you're terrible."

They both laughed as Auntie stirred her Bloody Mary with a celery stick. "Livvy," she said, "so how long has this been going on?"

"How long has what been going on?"

Auntie took a bite of the celery stick. "How long have you been sleeping with Chase?"

Liv took a big sip of her champagne.

"And Olivia, before you answer me, I know you would never lie to your dear, sweet aunt."

"You're right, Auntie. I wouldn't."

"Okay, so let's hear it. I need all of the details."

Liv gave in and spilled the juicy details to her aunt about her love affair with Chase.

"Well, Olivia, I must say, you certainly are in quite the pickle."

"No kidding, Auntie, and I really don't know what I'm going to do."

"Listen, kid, I gotta tell you, you're playing with fire. And Livvy, who else knows about this?"

"Just Beau and David. And now you."

"Look, Olivia, I really think you need to nip this romance in the bud."

Liv stared out at the ocean.

"Oh, boy," said Auntie, "the bud has already blossomed, hasn't it? Olivia, you're in love with him, aren't you?"

Liv nodded.

Auntie grabbed Liv's hand. "Well, Olivia, I think you're in for a bumpy ride with this one, but I get it. Just look at him. He's very sweet and extremely sexy. Do you know what I call that? That, my darling niece, is the deadly combo."

"He is, Auntie," said Liv, "and you're right."

"Well, Livvy, I could sit here all day until I'm blue in the face and list all of the reasons why this romance will never work out between the two of you, but, unfortunately, the heart wants what the heart wants."

Ain't that the truth? Liv thought. And Olivia Gallagher's heart wanted Chase Montgomery.

CHAPTER 25

A Cosmic Display

That night As Liv lay in bed, she thought back to the day's events. Her conversation with Auntie. Chase and her father enjoying a couple of beers as they took turns on the grill. Chase playing in the pool with Rose. And later in the afternoon, Chase scoring the winning touchdown in the family's beach football game. It certainly had turned out to be the perfect day and there was no doubt in Liv's mind that Chase had made a big splash with the entire Gallagher family.

Liv's mother had commented, "Liv, I must say Chase would be perfect for you if only he wasn't so young. How old is he again?"

"Thirty-one," Liv had replied.

"Oh, no, darling, unfortunately, that would never work. But at least you have a new friend." *A new friend?* Liv had thought. *If only she knew.*

Just as Liv reached over to turn off the lamp on her nightstand, she got a text: *Liv, I haven't had a single moment alone with you all day. Please meet me down on the beach. I heard on the news there's supposed to be meteor showers tonight. Chase XO.*

Liv smiled as she read the text. She replied, *Okay, you head down first, I'll wait 10 minutes and then I'll meet you down there. But we have to be very quiet, Chase, because Sandy will start barking if she hears us.*

No worries, Chase replied. *Heading down there now.*

Liv jumped out of bed and threw on her black sweatpants and black V-neck T-shirt. Her heart raced as she slowly crept down the creaky wooden staircase and carefully opened the front door. As she walked over the dune, she could see Chase waiting for her at the water's edge. He turned around and started walking toward her.

"I've missed you," he said as he spread a blanket out over the sand.

"Me, too," Liv replied as she took off her T-shirt and slipped off her sweat pants.

"You really are a wild one, Olivia Gallagher," laughed Chase.

"No, Chase, I'm just wild about you," Liv said as she pulled Chase's shirt up and over his head. She started kissing his neck as she unzipped his pants. She got down on her knees and began licking him very slowly. He began to groan with delight. Liv reached up and unbuttoned his pants and slid them off of him.

"Lay down," she whispered.

Chase lay down on his back and Liv straddled him. She leaned over and began kissing him as he caressed her breasts. She reached down and slid him inside of her.

"I've missed you," she whispered.

"You have no idea," Chase said as he reached up and flipped her over. She wrapped her legs around him as he moved slowly in and out of her. She reached up and grabbed his neck and began to passionately kiss him.

"I'm going to cum," she said.

"Me, too."

"Now, Chase," Liv screamed. "I'm going to cum now!" At that moment, Chase exploded inside of her.

"Damn, that was good," Liv said.

"No kidding," Chase said as he rolled over onto his back.

Liv put her head on his chest. "It just keeps getting better," she said as he made small circles with his fingers up and down her arm.

"Yes, it does. Hey, Liv, did you see that?"

"See what?"

"A shooting star."

Liv rolled over and looked up at the night sky as Chase held her in his arms. "Look, there's another one!" she said.

The sky lit up with dazzling streaks of light as they shot across the sky. "I've never seen anything like this," said Liv.

"Me neither," said Chase.

"And, Chase, just so you know, I've never felt this way about anyone before."

"Me neither, Liv."

So for the next few hours, Liv and Chase lay silently in each other's arms as the universe put on a magical cosmic display.

CHAPTER 26

Liv's Empty Nest

August 29th, 2015. Liv had been back on the island of Palm Beach for almost two weeks now. Austin and William had returned to Duke, and suddenly, Liv's bustling home was uncomfortably quiet. Liv cringed every time she walked past Austin and William's empty bedrooms. How she missed her sons.

Jeffrey could see his mother struggling and suggested that they change up their evening routine a bit. He'd said, "Mom, I think we should try to have dinner outside by the pool as much as possible." Kurt never allowed dinner to be served outside. He couldn't stand the heat and he always complained about the mosquitoes. "And after dinner, we should take nightly beach walks to look for shells and sea glass." Liv admired how Jeffrey was trying to help her, and their new nightly routine was actually making her quiet home seem somewhat bearable once again.

Thankfully, Beau was still calling her daily and coming over every Monday night for dinner. When Beau entered the house, Liv would always hug him and say, "Beau, I don't know what would I do without you. You truly are my sanity."

And luckily, Liv's relationship with Chase had continued to be a dream come true. Until the evening of September 3rd, that is.

Chase had texted Liv around noon that day and asked her if she could meet him for dinner at Ta-boo. She readily agreed and looked forward to another romantic evening with Chase.

When she arrived at the restaurant, Chase was waiting outside for her. They hugged and Chase said, "Sorry about the last-minute dinner invitation."

"No worries, handsome," said Liv, "I'm always excited to spend an evening with you. You know that."

They entered Ta-boo and the hostess led them to the back of the restaurant. She then seated them at their usual booth next to the fireplace. The waiter soon appeared, and Chase ordered a bottle of Veuve Clicquot and the fried oyster appetizer as well as the beef carpaccio.

"Chase, why did you order champagne?" asked Liv. "Are we celebrating something?"

Chase took Liv's hand. "No, Liv, not exactly. You see, something happened today at work that we need to talk about."

"Okay. So what happened?"

The waiter returned and poured them each a glass of champagne and said, "I'll be right back with your appetizers."

Chase took a large sip of his champagne. "So here's the thing, Liv. I have some bad news."

"Okay. Chase, what is it?"

"Morgan is transferring me back up to Atlanta."

"Wait—why?"

"Liv, please calm down and I'll explain everything to you. First of all, it's only temporary. The guy who took over my position is taking a six-month leave of absence because his wife has stage four breast cancer. Liv, the man's a wreck and he wants to be at home with his wife and four kids."

Liv took a sip of champagne. "Well, that's understandable," she said, "but why you?"

"Liv, it's my old position. I know that job inside and out. And besides, it's only for six months."

"So you're going?"

"Yes, Liv, I'm going."

Liv's heart dropped. "So when do you leave?"

"Next week. September 10th."

Liv couldn't believe this was happening. "Chase, what are we going to do? I mean, we see each other almost every day. And the thought of you leaving…" Her eyes filled and tears began to run down her cheeks.

Chase wiped her tears away and said, "Please, don't do that, Liv. You know how I hate to see you cry."

"Chase, I'm losing you, aren't I?"

"No, Liv. Don't be silly. I'm not going anywhere. And besides, people have long-distance relationships all the time. So please stop worrying. Liv, I know we can make this work."

"Promise?"

"Yes, Liv, I promise."

"I love you."

"I love you, too."

And at that moment, Liv hoped and prayed that her Prince Charming wasn't walking out of her life forever.

CHAPTER 27

Promises Made

September 9th, 2015. Liv was putting the final touches on her makeup when Ms. Dee walked into her bathroom with Rose. Over the summer, Liv had confessed her feelings for Chase to Ms. Dee.

"So, how are you holding up, Ms. Olivia?" asked Ms. Dee.

"Not that well, Ms. Dee," Liv replied, as her eyes filled with tears.

Ms. Dee reached out and took her hand. "Now please don't cry, Ms. Olivia. You'll ruin your makeup." She grabbed a tissue and carefully wiped away Liv's tears.

"I know, Ms. Dee," said Liv, "but I can't believe he's leaving. I love him more than anything, and after everything that Kurt has put me through, I'm finally happy."

"I know you are, Ms. Olivia. And Mr. Kurt was an idiot for walking out on you. You're a beautiful woman, Ms. Olivia, and a wonderful mother. But I do believe that the good Lord has sent you Mr. Chase. And the way he is with Rose is so very precious. So no more tears, Ms. Olivia. You need to go out tonight and have a wonderful evening. And then leave the rest in God's hands, okay?"

"Okay, Ms. Dee. And thank you."

At 6:00 sharp, Liv's doorbell rang. Rose ran ahead of Liv and opened the front door. Chase burst in and scooped Rose up in his arms.

"Boy, am I going to miss you," he said, as Liv and Ms. Dee looked on. "But don't worry. Remember what I told you. I'm going to call you every night at bedtime to say your prayers. And look, I got you a few things." Chase set Rose down and handed her a huge gift bag. Rose flung the pink tissue paper onto the floor and dug into the bag to discover a new backpack for school, Hello Kitty coloring books, and a Winnie the Pooh teddy bear.

"Thanks, Chase!" she said as she gave him a huge hug.

"Rose, I'm going to take your mommy out to dinner now, okay?" Rose nodded and gave Chase a kiss on the cheek.

"Are you ready to go, Liv?" asked Chase.

"Yes," Liv replied.

"Ms. Dee, please take good care of my girls for me, okay?"

"You bet, Mr. Chase," said Ms. Dee. "And I hope you get yourself back to the island real soon."

"Don't worry, Ms. Dee, that's my plan."

Chase opened Liv's car door for her and soon they were cruising up A1A with the top down. Chase glanced over at the ocean. "I'm sure going to miss seeing this every day. And your beautiful face, of course," he said as he kissed her hand.

Liv squeezed his hand hard as she fought back the tears.

Moments later, Liv said, "Chase, you just drove right past Al Fresco. Isn't our dinner reservation at 7:00?"

"No, Liv, not to worry. Our reservation isn't until 7:30. So I thought it would be nice to go for a little drive first, okay?" Liv nodded in agreement.

Soon, they were driving under a canopy of trees that covered a large stretch of A1A. Chase gradually slowed the car down, put on his hazard lights, and then put the car in park.

"Chase, what are you doing?"

Chase gazed up at the sky and said, "Liv, what does this remind you of?"

Liv looked up through the canopy of trees and spotted the first evening star.

"Sea Island, of course, where I first fell in love with you," she replied.

Chase reached into his pocket and pulled out a small wooden box. "Open it," he said as he handed her the box.

Liv carefully opened the box and inside, on a cream satin pillow, sat a platinum starfish diamond ring. Chase removed the ring and slid it onto Liv's finger.

"Liv, I understand that it's very hard for you to trust men after everything that Kurt has done to you, but you have to realize by now that I'm not him, and, Liv, if I ever make you a promise, just know that I intend to keep it. So while we're apart, if you're ever doubting me or our relationship, simply look down at your finger and know that I'm with you and I'm not going anywhere."

"Do you promise, Chase?" Liv asked.

"Yes, Liv, I promise," Chase replied.

Chase then leaned over and kissed Liv once again under a canopy of trees.

CHAPTER 28

He's Back

September, 2015. It had been a little over two weeks since Chase had moved back to Atlanta. Liv felt her heart shatter in a million pieces the day his U-Haul pulled out of the driveway. Every night since he'd left, she had cried herself to sleep. She missed everything about him—laying her head on his chest, the way her hand fit into his, the small circles he made with his fingers up and down her arm after they made love, and the kisses that always made her stomach do somersaults.

Liv had been in love many times throughout her life, but never like this. Chase was her best friend, partner, lover, and the soulmate she had been searching for her entire life. So once a week, she would send him a love letter along with a thoughtful care package.

For Liv, The time apart from Chase couldn't go by fast enough. But thankfully, Chase was doing all he could to make the separation between them bearable. Every morning, Liv would take a picture of the ocean on her beach walk and send it to Chase. As soon as he got the picture, he would call Liv on his drive into work. During his lunch break, Chase always checked in, and he would call her again on his way home. They would text throughout the evening and Chase, of course, did keep his promise to Rose; at 9:15 sharp, he would call her to say goodnight and to say prayers. And every Friday, he sent Liv a bouquet of her favorite flowers. Somehow, the distance that separated the two was actually making their love and commitment to each other stronger.

One day, when Liv was out on her morning walk, her cell phone rang. It was Abby Goldstein, her divorce attorney.

"Good morning, Abby. Is everything all right?" asked Liv.

"No, not really, Olivia. I need you to be in my office this afternoon at one o'clock."

"Okay, Abby, but what's this all about?"

"Don't worry, I'll explain everything to you this afternoon." And with that, she hung up.

At one o'clock sharp, Liv walked into Abby Goldstein's office. Liv put her purse down on the floor and took a seat.

Abby put her elbows on the desk and laced her fingers together.

"Olivia, we have a problem," she said.

"Okay," said Liv. "What is it?"

"You're not going to like this, but Kurt's back."

"What do you mean he's 'back'?"

"He's back from Europe. And he's asking for time-sharing with his children."

"What?! Are you kidding me? Abby, he just can't waltz back into their lives like this after he's been gone for over five months. And besides, Rose has finally settled into her new school routine, and she doesn't even ask for him anymore. I'm sorry, Abby, but This just isn't fair."

"Liv, try to calm down and listen to me. Whether you like it or not, he's their father and he has a right to see his children."

"After everything that he's done to all of us?! No, Abby, I don't think so."

"Look, Olivia, he has already filed a motion in court. And, unfortunately, he'll win. Now, I think it would be best to start off with Friday night dinners."

"What?!"

"He'll come to your house at five, pick up the kids, and have them back to you by nine."

"Kids?"

"Yes, Rose and Jeffrey."

"Kurt thinks Jeffrey is going to have dinner with him after everything that he's done? Abby, may I remind you that he drained that kid's bank account? Now, look, I realize that you've never met Jeffrey, but my son is six-four, 235 pounds. All muscle. I'd like to see a judge, or his father, force him to do anything."

"Okay, okay," said Abby, "I will speak to his attorney about Jeffrey, but Rose has to go. And listen, Olivia, he's also asking for every other weekend—Friday through Tuesday. But I got him to agree to start with this."

"Oh, my God! He's going to take her every other weekend? Abby, there must be something you can do."

"Olivia, my hands are tied, and, unfortunately, these are his rights under the law. But look, we're just going to start off with the Friday night dinners for now, okay?"

"No, Abby, none of this is okay. But I guess I really don't have a choice now, do I?"

"Olivia, what can I say, except 'welcome to the land of divorce'? Oh, and one last thing. We've finally scheduled mediation."

"Okay, when is it?"

"October 20th."

"Are you kidding me?"

"Why? Is there a problem?"

"Yes, there's a problem. That's my birthday! And I'm supposed to go up to Atlanta to spend the weekend with Chase."

"Well, Olivia, you're just going to have to change your plans because you'll be in mediation that day. And may I remind you that the mediation is a court order. Also, Olivia, as your legal counsel, I really think you should end things with Chase. I mean, let's face it, you had a nice summer romance, but now, it's time to get serious."

Liv's heart was pounding and her head was spinning. It had taken her five months to get her and her children's lives back to some kind of normalcy.

"Abby, I appreciate your legal advice, but from now on, my personal life is off limits. Is that understood?"

"Olivia, I'm telling you, you're making a big mistake, and I'm just trying to look out for you."

"So, when do these Friday dinners start?"

"This week. September 25th."

Liv stood up, grabbed her purse, and stormed out of the office. When she got into her car, tears began rolling down her face. As she turned on the car's ignition, she thought, *I can't believe this monster is back in my life!*

CHAPTER 29

Friday Dinners

On Liv's drive home from Abby's office, she made several phone calls—to her parents, kids, Chase, and Beau—to fill them in on her new time-sharing schedule with Kurt.

Her mother was appalled. "Liv, can he legally do this?" she asked.

"Yes, Mom," Liv replied. "Apparently, it's his legal right to see Rose whether we like it or not."

"Olivia, this is just awful, and I feel so sorry for Rose."

"So do I, Mom. I finally got her adjusted to our new routine, and now this."

"Well Liv, you're just going to have to make this as easy as possible for her."

"I know, Mom, and of course, I'm going to try, but I really can't believe this is happening."

When William and Austin heard the news, they were both very relieved that they were away at college. "That man is dead to me," declared William. Austin had said, "Mom, I'm so sorry you're going through all of this, but I just don't have any good feelings left for him anymore."

When Jeffrey heard about the time-sharing, he said, "Mom, if you think there's a rat's chance in hell that I'd go to dinner with that clown, you're out of your mind."

"Okay, Jeffrey. Please try to calm down, and I promise to pass your wishes along to my attorney," Liv had said, "but I think you should make plans on Friday nights from now on if you truly don't want to see your father."

"Oh, don't worry, Mom," said Jeffrey. "I definitely won't be here."

"So what time does the prick come over on Fridays?" Beau had asked.

"He'll be here every Friday at five," Liv told him.

"Well, Love, I guess from now on, we'll be having dinner at your house on Friday nights."

"Beau, What are you saying?"

"Love, do you really think I'm going to let you be alone with that asshole?"

"Wow, Beau, I can't thank you enough."

"Sure you can. You can cook me one hell of a dinner every Friday night."

"Okay, Beau, you've got yourself a deal, and I promise to make you whatever you want."

When Chase heard of the time-sharing schedule, he had said, "Oh, Liv, I really wish I was back in Palm Beach."

"Me too," said Liv.

"And, Liv, I thought I would never say this, but I'm so glad Beau has agreed to be there. It definitely is a big load off my mind, and it does speak volumes about his character."

"I know, Chase, it really does. And to be honest, I don't know what I would do without the two of you."

Friday, September 25th. Liv was getting Rose dressed for her first dinner with Kurt.

"So, Rose, are you excited to go out to dinner with your daddy tonight?" she asked as she zipped up Rose's Lilly Pulitzer shift.

Rose had a confused look on her face. "Mommy, where are we going for dinner?" she asked.

"I'm not really sure. And remember, I told you I wasn't coming to dinner tonight. This is just a special dinner for you and Daddy. But don't worry. I'm sure he's going to take you somewhere fun."

"But I want you to come, Mommy."

Just then, Liv heard, "Oh, honey, I'm home!"

Oh God, she thought. *It's Kurt.* She looked down at her watch: 4:45. *Damn, he's early, and where the hell is Beau? Okay, Olivia. You can do this*, Liv told herself as she took in a deep breath and grabbed Rose's hand. "Let's go see your daddy."

As Rose and Liv walked down the main staircase, Kurt was waiting for them at the bottom holding a bouquet of red roses and a Hello Kitty stuffed animal.

"Well, there are my two beautiful girls," he said. He handed Liv the bouquet and then bent down to pick up Rose. Liv was at a loss for words and Rose looked as if she was going to burst into tears at any moment.

"Rose, why don't you go and put the Hello Kitty up in your room so I can talk to your daddy for a minute?" suggested Liv.

Kurt carefully put Rose down. She then grabbed the Hello Kitty, ran up the stairs, and slammed her bedroom door. Liv couldn't help noticing that Kurt was wearing his wedding band. *Why on earth is he still wearing that?* she thought.

"Okay, Kurt, First of all, you have no right to walk into my home. From now on, I want you to wait in your car and I will bring Rose out to you. And please don't bring me any gifts. It's completely inappropriate," she said as she handed him back the roses.

Kurt laughed. "Liv, I don't know who the hell you think you are, but this is still my house and you are still legally my wife," he said as he placed the roses down on a table in the foyer. "And by the way, when did your skirts get so short? I hate to tell you, Liv, but you're leaving very little to the imagination."

Outside, Beau peeled into Liv's driveway. He jumped out of his truck and raced into the house.

"Love," he said out of breath, "I'm so sorry I'm late. There was a huge accident on 95."

"Kurt, I'd like you to meet Beau Walker," said Liv.

Beau reached out his hand but Kurt laughed and said, "If you think I'm shaking hands with the man who's screwing my wife, you're out of your mind."

Liv looked up and saw Rose standing at the top of the stairs.

"Rose, please come down here now. I don't want you and Daddy to be late for dinner."

Rose slowly walked down the stairs. "But I want to stay here and have dinner with you and Beau, Mommy," she said as she clung to Liv's legs.

Kurt bent down, picked up Rose, and said, "Come on, my little princess, we're going to Tessa's for fried chicken and strawberry pie."

And with that, he was out the door. Liv fell into Beau's arms and began to sob.

Friday, October 2nd, 4:45. Liv and Rose were standing on the front porch waiting for Kurt's arrival. After the uncomfortable events of last week's pick-up, Liv spoke to her attorney and a new protocol was now in place. Kurt was to stay in his car and Liv would bring Rose out to him. He was also no longer permitted to enter Liv's home. Beau, on the other hand, was allowed to be there, but was instructed to stay in the house to avoid any future conflicts with Kurt. Liv's attorney also advised Liv to make the exchanges as brief as possible for Rose's sake.

At 4:50, Kurt pulled into the driveway in his black Mercedes AMG GT 63 four-door sedan. Liv and Rose walked toward the car. Kurt got out and said, "How's my little princess doing today?"

He bent down to pick Rose up, but she said nothing. Liv kissed Rose on the cheek and said, "Go have fun with Daddy and I'll see you back here real soon."

Kurt turned and buckled Rose into her car seat. Liv began to walk away, but she couldn't help herself.

"Kurt, wait." She walked over to him and grabbed his left hand. "Why on earth are you still wearing this?" she said, touching his wedding band.

"It's none of your damn business."

"Kurt, It's not healthy. Listen, why don't you give me the ring so I can put it in the safety deposit box? Who knows, maybe one of the boys might want it someday."

"No, Olivia, it's fine where it is."

"Kurt, you make no sense. You're the one who left me, remember, and now you're acting like the victim. Can you please tell me why you did what you did? Kurt, I need and deserve an explanation."

But Kurt said nothing. He turned around, got into his car, and drove away.

169

Friday, October 9th, 4:45. Once again, Liv and Rose were on the front porch waiting for Kurt's arrival. But Liv had learned her lesson from last week's exchange. She now knew that she was never going to get any answers out of Kurt and she just needed to let it all go. At 4:55, Liv saw Kurt pull up in front of her mailbox out on the street. She took Rose's hand and began to walk toward the car.

"My attorney advised me not to pull into the driveway," said Kurt as he got out of the car. He opened the back door and buckled Rose into her car seat. "Meet me back out here at 9:00 sharp," he commanded.

"Okay," said Liv. Kurt turned, got back into the car, and sped off.

What's gotten into him? thought Liv.

Later that evening, she and Beau were enjoying another fabulous Friday night dinner out by the pool.

"Love, you've truly outdone yourself tonight," said Beau. "Your roasted chicken and whipped potatoes are out of this world."

"Thanks, Beau. And thanks again for coming over."

"You don't need to thank me, Love. I'm happy to be here, you know that. And besides, I must say your ex-husband is one weird dude."

"You're telling me. One minute he's nice the, next minute…oh, well, it doesn't matter as long as Rose is okay."

"So how was Rose today?"

"Well, as you know, the first two dinners were rough. A lot of tears. But today was a little better. By the way, Beau, what time is it? I don't want to be late meeting him."

Beau looked down at his watch and said, "Don't worry, Love. It's only 8:30."

Just then, the two heard a booming voice from across the yard.

"Well, would you look at this romantic scene?" said Kurt.

Liv stood up immediately and said, "Rose, go upstairs, brush your teeth, put on your pajamas, and I'll be right up to tuck you in."

Rose turned and ran into the house.

"Kurt, what the hell are you doing?" asked Liv. "I'm supposed to meet you out front, remember?"

Kurt walked over to the table carrying a bouquet of sunflowers and examined the dinner table. "I see you made this asshole my favorite meal. Her roasted chicken is almost as tasty as her pussy, wouldn't you say so, Beau?" Kurt threw the flowers down on the table and stormed out of the yard.

Friday, October 16th, 4:45. Liv and Rose were standing out by the mailbox once again waiting for Kurt's arrival. At five o'clock, he pulled up and rolled down the window of his car. "Can you put her in this time?" he asked.

Liv nodded. She then opened the car door and buckled Rose into her car seat. "Have a good time, Rose," she said as she kissed her on the forehead. As soon as she closed the car door, Kurt took off.

Liv had informed Abby Goldstein about the outlandish events of last week's exchange and she, in turn, had composed a very stern letter to Kurt's attorney. *I guess he's pissed off about the letter*, Liv thought as she walked back into the house.

At 8:45, Liv was standing out by the mailbox waiting for Kurt. Beau was in the kitchen loading the dishwasher after another lovely dinner. At 9:15, Kurt finally pulled up and rolled down his window.

"Can you get her out?" he asked.

"Sure, but Kurt, if you're going to be late, I'd appreciate a text," Liv replied. She then opened the back door and as she went to unbuckle Rose, Kurt grabbed her arm.

"Don't tell me what to do, you filthy whore," he seethed as he slowly pushed down on the accelerator. Liv's bare feet were being dragged across the rough pavement.

"Let go of me!" Liv shouted. "Kurt, let go!" She was now screaming at the top of her lungs. Rose began to wail. "Stop the car, Kurt! Stop!" Liv managed to grab a shopping bag off of the back seat with her free hand. She began hitting him over the head repeatedly as hard as she could until he finally let go. She eventually fell to her knees in the road as Beau came running down the street. Kurt jumped out of the car, ran around the other side, and took Rose out of the car. He then got back in the car and sped away.

"Oh my God, Liv, what the hell happened?" Beau asked, holding his cell phone up to his ear.

"Yes," he said to the 911 operator, "there's been a domestic dispute at 145 Seaspray Avenue and we need police assistance ASAP!"

The next morning, Liv was at the Palm Beach County Courthouse filling out the necessary paperwork for a restraining order. Her hands shook as she wrote down on paper the events of the night before. She signed and dated the signature page, praying she would never have to see Kurt ever again. But unfortunately, Liv knew in her heart that Kurt had no intentions of letting her go. Not now, not ever.

CHAPTER 30

Mediation

October 20th, 9:00 a.m. Liv stepped into the elevator with Abby Goldstein, hardly believing that this was how she was going to be spending her forty-first birthday. Chase, of course, had been very understanding and sweet when he heard she couldn't come up to Atlanta for the weekend. "No worries, Liv," he had said. "We'll find another weekend to celebrate your birthday. And just think, you're one step closer to finally being divorced and rid of that lunatic forever."

Earlier that morning, Beau had called her and said, "Give 'em hell, Love. And don't worry, I'll be waiting at your house to take you out for a nice birthday dinner when this is all over."

In the elevator, Liv asked Abby, "Are you sure I'm not going to have to see him today?"

"Don't worry, Olivia," Abby replied. "The mediator is well aware of your restraining order and he has taken every precaution to make sure that you feel safe and comfortable today. So, you'll be in one conference room with me and Kurt will be in another conference room with his attorney. The mediator will simply go back and forth."

When Liv stepped out of the elevator, her hands began to sweat and her heart began to race. As soon as they entered the mediation office, the receptionist greeted them. "Good morning, Mrs. Goldstein," she said. "If you'll please follow me, I'll show you to your conference room."

Abby and Liv followed behind her. But as they came around the corner of the hallway, there stood Kurt. Liv immediately stopped. Abby turned to her and said, "Go back and wait in the lobby while I take care of this."

Liv nodded. Tears welled up in her eyes as she walked back to the lobby. Just the sight of Kurt made her tremble. *How am I ever going to get through this day?* she thought.

Finally, Abby returned and said, "We're going to be on the other side of the office, so this won't happen again. So please don't worry, Olivia, I took care of it. Okay?"

Liv nodded.

Once in their conference room, Abby began taking out legal pads, pens, bottled waters, and snacks from her oversized tote bag.

"My goodness, Abby, you're acting as if we're going to be locked up in here for days," said Liv.

"Listen, my little sweet potato," said Abby, "Your ex-husband is a slippery, slimy snake, and if you think today is going to be a piece of cake, you're greatly mistaken. And, Olivia, I'm telling you, If we get out of here before midnight, it will be a true miracle."

Just then, Liv's two forensic accountants walked in followed by Abby's paralegal.

"Well, let's all get comfortable," Abby said as she passed out the bottled waters. "So as you all know, I've been doing this for over thirty years now, and I'm telling you, this is going to be one hell of a long day."

Douglas McDade, the mediator, soon entered the room. He introduced himself and then took a seat next to Liv.

"Olivia," he said, "I just met with Kurt, and to start the day off, I asked him to write down three remarkable things about you." Mr.

McDade unfolded a piece of paper. "But I'm happy to report he actually wrote down ten: 'Liv is beautiful, a great mother, loving, a gifted teacher, a good friend, sweet, kind, funny, selfless, and very loyal.' So now, Olivia, I would like you to write down three positive qualities about Kurt."

Liv picked up the pen he handed her and stared down at the blank sheet of paper. After about three minutes, she put the pen down and handed Mr. McDade back the piece of paper.

"Olivia, I don't understand," Mr. McDade said. "Are you telling me you don't have one good thing to say about Kurt? Now come on, Olivia, you were married to the man for twenty-one years. You must have something nice to say about him."

Liv sat back in her chair and crossed her arms. She glared at Mr. McDade and said, "Mr. McDade, are you aware of how my husband left me?" Mr. McDade shook his head. "Well, let me fill you in. He planned a very elaborate twentieth anniversary celebration the night before he left at The Breakers Hotel. And over dinner, he told me that I was his best friend and the love of his life. After dinner we went up to our hotel room and had sex all night. The next morning, when I woke up, he was gone, and when I arrived back to our home, much to my surprise, I was served divorce papers. At noon, the electricity and the cable went out. I tried to use my credit cards to get the power back on, but none of them worked. That same day, he drained all of our bank accounts: Our joint accounts, the kids' accounts, even my charity organization's account! I only had thirty-eight dollars in my wallet, that was it. He then ran off to Europe for over five months, leaving me behind to handle all of our financial responsibilities and to raise our four children alone. So, no, Mr. McDade, as a matter of fact, I *don't* have one good thing to say about the monster who is currently sitting down the hall."

"I'm sorry, Mrs. Donovan," said Mr. McDade, "and I honestly don't know what to say. I've been a mediator for over twenty years now and I've never had a spouse hand me back a blank piece of paper."

Abby interrupted. "Douglas, excuse my language, but the man's a piece of shit. So let's just try to get through the day the best we can."

Mr. McDade nodded, folded up the blank piece of paper, and walked out of the room.

The next few hours were filled with heated conversations regarding the family home, the contents of the home, marital gifts, and of course, time-sharing with Rose. At noon, they all decided to take an hour-long lunch break. The receptionist came in and passed out menus and began taking lunch orders. When she got to Liv she said, "Oh, I already have your order."

"Excuse me?" Liv said.

"Mr. Donovan said you'll have the chicken salad platter with a side of ranch dressing."

"Are you kidding me? You can go tell that asshole that he can no longer make any decisions regarding me, including what I eat for lunch! Is that clear?"

The receptionist nodded and quickly left the room.

"Okay, Olivia," said Abby, "let's all try to calm down, shall we? After the lunch break, you're going to have to decide if you're willing to buy him out of the family home for the $3.35 million that he's asking for."

Liv looked down at her purse and thought about the blank checks that her mother had sent to her and the conversation that they'd had.

"Olivia," her mother had said, "I am overnighting you a few blank checks from Gallagher Construction to take with you to mediation. I want you to promise me that you'll do whatever's necessary to protect the children. My poor grandchildren have been through enough, and they certainly don't need any more crosses to bear. So, if during the course of the mediation money becomes an issue, which I'm sure it will, give the asshole whatever he wants in order to protect the children."

Liv quietly removed one of the checks from her purse and filled it out. $3.35 million. "Here," she said as she passed the check over to Abby.

Abby looked down at the check. "Are you sure about this, Olivia?"

"Yes. I don't want my children to have to leave their family home after everything that they've already been through. But I do have a few requests. I want the contents of the house, and I mean *everything*. Every stick of furniture, every plate, cup, fork. Everything in the house is now mine. Also, I want the conditions of my restraining order to remain in place even after it expires. Which means he is still not allowed to call or text me. The only way he can communicate with me is through emails, and it must be in regards to Rose. Finally, there must be a new designated location for drop-off and pick-up. I don't want that animal anywhere near my home ever again after what he did to me. And trust me, I will never go to another drop-off or pick-up as long as I live. A caregiver or a friend will meet him from now on. Is this all clear?"

Abby picked up the check and said, "Okay, let me go see what I can do."

Thirty minutes later, she returned. "Well, what do you know?" she said. "He took the money."

No surprise there, thought Liv.

"But he does want his clothes. Nothing else, just his clothes. Oh, and also his watches and his gun collection. He did ask for the extensive wine collection, but I said no shot. Can you accept these terms?"

"Yes," Liv replied, "but as you know, I don't want to be alone with him ever again."

"Not to worry, Olivia. I'll make sure the police are present on the day he comes to collect all of his belongings."

At that point, Mr. McDade came back into the conference room.

"Okay, so let's talk about time-sharing with Rose now," he said. "Kurt wants Monday and Wednesday dinners, and every other weekend. He also wants all the holidays on even years—Thanksgiving, Christmas, et cetera. The same goes for spring break and winter break."

"I think I'm going to vomit," Liv said. The thought of not having Rose on Christmas morning, or her not sitting next to her at the dining room table on Thanksgiving was just too much to bear. She said, "I'm sorry, but this is not acceptable to me. The man leaves for over five months and has not even tried to see Rose until recently, and now he's going to pull this shit? I'm sorry, but it's just plain wrong!"

"Douglas," said Abby, "can I please have a moment alone with my client?"

Mr. McDade nodded and left the room.

"Look, Olivia," said Abby, "I told you this was going to happen. Like it or not, he's Rose's father and he has rights. Also, this is a game to him. The more time he spends with Rose, the less he'll have to pay you in child support."

"What if I don't want child support?" asked Liv. "If it means Rose spends the majority of her time with me, then let him keep his damn money."

"Olivia, he has to pay you child support. It's the law."

Liv thought about the other checks in her purse. She put her arms on the table and laced her fingers. "What if I offer him $50,000 so I can make the time-sharing schedule?"

"Olivia, have you lost your mind?"

"Abby, listen to me. I know him, and believe me, this is not about Rose; this is all about the money. And don't worry, I promise to be reasonable with him, but I'm going to make a schedule that won't turn my little girl's world upside down!"

Just then, Mr. McDade came back into the room.

"Mr. McDade, I've come up with an idea," said Liv.

"Olivia, I'm telling you, this is a big mistake," interrupted Abby.

"Abby, I have to do what's best for my daughter. Mr. McDade, I am willing to offer Mr. Donovan $50,000 in order for me to make the time-sharing schedule. Now, I promise to be fair with him, but the schedule on the table right now is very disruptive to my daughter, so please go back over there and see if he'll agree to what I'm suggesting."

"Olivia, I'll do what you've asked," said Mr. McDade, "but I can assure you that Kurt is never going to take the money. He told me Rose is his whole world."

"Mr. McDade," said Liv, "I can promise you that he will most definitely take the money."

"Okay, I'll go and present him with your offer."

As Mr. McDade turned to leave, Liv secretly hoped that she was wrong about Kurt. But in less than fifteen minutes, Mr. McDade walked back into the room.

"Okay, Olivia, he's agreed to your terms."

What an ass, thought Liv as she filled out the check. As she handed the check over to Mr. McDade she said, "I believe Mr. Donovan has just shown you his true colors."

The next three hours were spent drafting the divorce agreement and trying to sort out child support. Kurt's current financial affidavit showed that he was making $75,000 a year. As Liv looked over Kurt's paperwork, she said, "This can't be right. He was making close to a million dollars for at least the last five years."

Mr. Kellogg, one of Liv's forensic accountants, explained. "Olivia, we have tried for five months to find more assets and income, but unfortunately, we've come up with nothing."

Abby interrupted, "Olivia, as we all now know, Kurt hired his attorney a year-and-a-half ago, so he had plenty of time to hide his money."

"So basically," said Liv, "what you're all telling me is that Kurt is smarter than everyone who is sitting around this table." She glanced up at the clock: 4:45. *Lord, we've been here for almost eight hours now,* she thought.

In a short while, Mr. McDade walked in.

"Here's where we're at," he said. "Kurt is willing to give you $600 a month, and he's also willing to cover Jeffrey and Rose's health insurance."

"That's it?" Liv asked.

"Yes. Oh, and he knows it's your birthday, so he suggested that we order dinner from the Italian restaurant across the street."

"Are you fucking kidding me?" said Liv. "Here's the deal: I have dinner plans, so when that clock strikes 6:00, I'm out of here. Now, go tell my soon-to-be ex-husband to throw in his $2 million life insurance policy so we can all get the hell out of here."

Mr. McDade grabbed the paperwork and left the room.

"Abby," said Liv, "I really need to be getting out of here. I mean, it's bad enough that I'm getting royally screwed on my birthday, but at least let me go and have a nice birthday dinner."

"Okay," said Abby. "Let me go see if I can get this done."

Abby left the conference room and Liv began flipping through Kurt's financial affidavit. *Lies,* she thought. *This whole thing is a bunch of lies. Just like our marriage.*

"Olivia, you did a good job today," said Mr. Kellogg.

"Well, it sure doesn't feel like it."

"Listen, you put Rose and your other children first. You're a fantastic mother and a wonderful woman. You should be very proud of what you did here today. I'm just sorry I couldn't have done more."

Liv nodded, and soon Abby returned with the final draft of their divorce agreement.

"Okay, Olivia. Just initial every page, and then sign the last page, and you're free to go."

Liv flipped through the documents and signed as fast as she could, and then handed them back to Abby.

"Come on, I'll walk you out," said Abby.

When they reached the lobby, there stood Kurt with his legal team.

"I heard you were in a rush to leave because you have a hot date," said Kurt.

Liv looked at Abby.

"Just go, Olivia," said Abby. "Have a wonderful birthday. And you are now officially a *free* woman."

Liv hugged Abby and strode out of the office. She could hear arguing as she walked down the hallway. When she stepped into the elevator her eyes filled with tears. *Free*, she thought. But somehow, in her heart, she doubted that she would ever be free of Kurt Donovan.

CHAPTER 31

Diamonds on the Day of Your Divorce

When the elevator doors opened, much to Liv's surprise there stood Beau wearing a navy-blue pinstripe suit and a pale pink dress shirt.

"Beau, what on earth are you doing here?"

"Well, Love, when it got to be past five o'clock, I decided I'd better come down here to make sure you were all right," Beau replied. "So, how did it go?"

"Beau, I feel like I've been through a war."

Beau extended his arm. "Well, Love, I think it's time to get this birthday celebration underway. Don't you?"

"Sounds good to me," said Liv, "but first I have to get my car from the valet."

"No need, Love. I had Ms. Dee come down here and take your car back to the house for you."

"Thanks, Beau. You really do always take the best care of me," she said as she climbed up into Beau's truck. "So, Mr. Walker, where are you taking me for my birthday dinner?"

"Tonight, we will be dining at Kathy's Gazebo."

Liv thought back to the last time she was there with Kurt. They didn't even make it through the appetizer course.

"Beau, why did you choose Kathy's Gazebo?" she asked.

"So last week, I decided to text the boys separately to get their input on your birthday dinner and they all told me, 'Take her to Kathy's Gazebo. She loves it there.'"

"Well, that's definitely true," said Liv, "but the last time I was there, it was a complete disaster. You see, Kurt announced that he had decided to take a job with the CIA up in DC and would only be coming home on the weekends for the next two years. Needless to say, that didn't sit very well with me."

"I bet, Love. But not to worry," said Beau. "Tonight you're dining with me, so I know you're going to have a fabulous time." Then he reached over and kissed her hand.

When they arrived at the restaurant, Beau pulled his truck up to the valet stand and then quickly walked around to open Liv's door.

Inside, the maître d' hugged Liv.

"Olivia!" he said. "Where have you been?"

"Claude, to say that these last few years have been rough would be a huge understatement," Liv replied. "And I guess you haven't heard, but Kurt and I aren't together anymore. Anyways, enough of all that. Claude, I would like you to meet my dear friend, Beau Walker."

"Good to meet you, Mr. Walker," said Claude. "And, sir, I want you to know that you're dining with a very special lady this evening."

"Claude, believe me, I already know," Beau nodded. "She truly is one of a kind, and tonight's her birthday."

"Oh, Olivia, happy birthday! I'm so glad you chose the Gazebo for your birthday celebration. And if you will both please follow me, I have the perfect table for the two of you." Claude quickly showed them to a cozy, candlelit corner booth. He then handed them each a dinner menu and placed the wine list on the table.

"Enjoy!" he said as he kissed Liv's hand.

"Beau, please excuse me for a minute. I want to go freshen up in the lady's room real quick," said Liv.

"Of course. Take your time."

Liv touched up her foundation, then gently dabbed on her finishing powder and reapplied her lipstick. *What a day*, she thought as she looked in the mirror.

When she returned to the table she saw a black velvet box resting on her dinner plate along with a single, long-stem red rose.

"Beau, what's this?"

"Just open it, Love," Beau replied.

Liv carefully opened the box. Inside was a stunning diamond and sapphire channel band.

"You see, Love, I decided that you should have diamonds on the day of your divorce."

"Beau, I can't believe you did this!"

Beau picked up the ring and slid it gently onto Liv's finger. He then raised his champagne glass and said, "Happy birthday, Love, and cheers to new beginnings!"

Liv looked down at her finger and then into Beau's beautiful blue eyes and thought, *I do wonder what the future has in store for me...*

CHAPTER 32

"He Didn't Take Anything!"

November 4th, 2015. The day that Liv had been dreading had finally arrived. At two o'clock, Kurt was coming to the house to pick up his clothes, watches, and gun collection. As Abby had promised, officers from the Palm Beach County Police Department would be stationed outside and throughout the home.

Abby also suggested to Liv that she should have a male friend present to make her feel more comfortable and to ensure that everything went smoothly. Since Chase was still up in Atlanta, Liv had asked Beau to be at the house. "Well, of course, Love," he had responded when she'd asked. "Anything for you. You know that."

At 1:45, the police arrived at Liv's home. They quickly positioned themselves in the front foyer, in the hallway outside of Liv's bedroom, and in the driveway. Shortly afterward, Kurt pulled into the driveway in a pickup truck. He grabbed some boxes out of the bed of the truck and then greeted the officers.

"Sorry you fellas have to be here today," he said. "What can I say? The woman is bat shit crazy." Kurt entered the home, bounded up the main staircase, and opened the door to the master bedroom. Liv sat nervously on the edge of the bed and Beau was seated at a table out on the master bedroom's balcony.

"What the fuck is he doing here?" Kurt asked when he saw Beau.

Liv stood up, crossed her arms, and said, "My attorney told me I was allowed to have a friend present."

"Olivia, let's face it, he's not a friend. He's just another one of your boy toys. And once again, you are dressed up like a whore. Liv, may I remind you that you are a mother of four, so maybe you should start dressing more appropriately."

Liv glanced out at Beau who was looking down at his phone.

Kurt went into the closet and started to throw his clothes into the boxes. Then he came back into the bedroom and began grabbing framed family photos.

"Kurt, you're not allowed to take those," said Liv. "The court order states you can only take your clothes, watches, and gun collection."

"Shut up, you stupid cunt," said Kurt. "I'm taking whatever I damn well please."

"Kurt, I will not allow you to speak to me that way. Do you understand me?"

Beau slowly put his phone down and walked into the bedroom.

"Kurt," he said, "I suggest you pack up all of your shit and get the hell out of her house."

"Oh, so you think you can tell me what to do? Fuck you!"

Liv quickly ran out of the bedroom and grabbed the police officer who was stationed in the hallway.

"Why aren't you doing anything?" she asked.

"Listen, Mrs. Donovan," said the police officer, "you really need to calm down. And by the way, having another man here was a big mistake on your part. You're flat-out antagonizing him."

"Oh, so you're on his side!" said Liv. "Listen, you need to tell him that according to the court order he has exactly forty-five minutes left to pack up all his things." Liv thought back to all the times Kurt had stopped by the police department and handed out free equipment. *The cops are in his pocket*, she decided.

When she walked back into the bedroom, Kurt grabbed Beau by his shirt and spit in his face.

"The little whore is all yours, buddy," Kurt said as he kicked a box across the room and then stormed out.

Liv ran across the room and hugged Beau.

"Are you okay? I'm so sorry!"

"I'm fine, Love."

Liv looked around the room. "Beau, he didn't take anything." She raced down the main staircase and out to the driveway. She went up to the first officer she saw and said, "He didn't take anything?"

"Apparently not, Mrs. Donovan," the officer replied.

Kurt peeled out of the driveway, giving Liv the middle finger as he drove away.

The following week, Abby instructed Liv to drop off all of Kurt's clothes at a Goodwill store, to put his watch collection in her safe deposit box, and to turn his gun collection over to the Palm Beach County PD. Liv followed Abby's instructions to the letter. When she returned home and saw Kurt's empty closet for the first time, she finally felt as though she could breathe again. *He's gone and he can't hurt me anymore*, she thought as she closed the closet doors and quietly walked out of her bedroom.

CHAPTER 33

The Magic of Christmas

D ecember 16th, 2015. The holiday season was in full swing on the island of Palm Beach. Liv had decked the halls of her beautiful home, and the family's twelve-foot-tall Christmas tree stood majestically in the formal living room. Liv was busy in the kitchen preparing dinner for that evening—roasted chicken, her mother's world-famous scalloped potatoes, green beans almondine, and, for dessert, her legendary Jelly Belly Christmas cookies.

Jeffrey was out of town for the weekend with the school's traveling basketball team, and Austin and William were still away at college. So tonight, it would just be Liv, Chase, and Rose for dinner. Liv had meticulously set the dining room table with her Spode Christmas China and matching wine goblets. She had also polished her grandmother's silver candelabras until they sparkled, and, last but not least, she placed the traditional Christmas centerpiece on the table. It was composed of red roses, carnations, white Asiatic lilies, pine cones, and assorted Christmas greenery. She then turned on the gas fireplace in the dining room and made sure the sounds of Christmas carols filled the air. This was by far Liv's favorite time of year, and she couldn't wait to celebrate Christmas 2015 with Chase.

At six o'clock sharp, the doorbell rang. Liv and Rose rushed to the door in their matching red plaid Vineyard Vine dresses. Chase walked into the foyer wearing navy dress slacks with a Brooks Brothers navy blazer and a red and white gingham dress shirt. His arms were loaded down with shopping bags and two bouquets of roses.

"Chase, what's all this?" asked Liv. "Christmas is still ten days away."

"I know," Chase replied, "but I thought it would be nice to have Rose open my gifts for her tonight, if that's okay with you."

"Please, Mommy, please?!" Rose exclaimed as she jumped up and down.

"Okay, Rose," said Liv, "after dinner, you can open the presents."

At 6:30, the three of them sat down to enjoy Liv's carefully prepared meal.

"Liv, you have truly outdone yourself tonight," said Chase. "This dinner is spectacular."

"Well, Mr. Montgomery, I'm glad you now realize that you're not the only one who knows their way around the kitchen," Liv replied with a wink.

"Liv, After tonight's dinner I promise to never doubt your cooking skills ever again," Chase said. He then raised his wine glass. "Cheers to my two beautiful girls." They all three touched glasses and Rose giggled as she took a sip of her ginger ale out of her champagne glass.

After dinner, they gathered around the Christmas tree. Liv poured two glasses of champagne and placed a platter of Jelly Bellies on the coffee table. Chase picked up a raspberry jam cookie and took a bite.

"Wow, Liv, what's in these? They're fantastic."

"Love and a little bit of Christmas magic," Liv replied.

Liv sat down on the sofa next to Chase and they both watched as Rose joyfully opened one Christmas present after another.

Chase leaned over and kissed Liv.

"Welcome home, handsome," she said, and they kissed again.

"I love you, Liv."

"I love you too."

"Liv," Chase added, "I promise to make this the best Christmas of your life."

"Chase, you being home is the only Christmas gift I need or want this year."

"Well, maybe I have a little Christmas magic of my own up my sleeves."

"Mr. Montgomery, do you have a surprise for me? What is it? I love surprises."

"I guess you'll just have to wait and see," Chase smiled, and then he kissed her again.

Four days later, Liv was standing at the reception desk at the Eau Spa. As an early Christmas gift, Chase had booked her a full day of pampering.

"Welcome to the Eau," said the receptionist.

"Thank you. It's great to be back."

"And what services are you having done today?"

"To tell you the truth, I'm really not sure. My boyfriend surprised me with a spa day."

"Well, that was awfully sweet of him. And what is your name?"

"Olivia—"

"Oh, yes, here it is," said the receptionist before Liv could finish. "Olivia Montgomery."

Liv smiled thinking to herself what a nice ring the name had.

"So it looks as though your boyfriend has booked you a massage, a facial, manicure, pedicure, blowout, and makeup application," said the receptionist.

"Wow, are you sure?"

"Oh, yes, I'm quite sure. Now, if you'll please follow Sandra, she'll show you to the ladies locker room."

After Liv had changed into her spa robe and slippers, she sat in the solarium, sipping on a glass of champagne and nibbling on a mini chocolate cupcake, which was to die for. She put her feet up on the ottoman and closed her eyes and thought, *This sure isn't a bad way to spend the day.*

Soon, the spa attendant called her name and showed her to one of the treatment rooms. For the next four hours, Liv was pampered from head to toe. Then the spa attendant reappeared to say, "I'm ready to take you over to the salon now for your blowout and makeup application."

"You know, I think I'll save that for another time," Liv said. "I'm just going home after this, so I don't really need my hair and makeup done today."

The spa attendant smiled and said, "He thought you might say that." Then she handed Liv a small notecard. Liv opened it. *Liv, Christmas is a time for magical surprises. See you soon, Chase XO.*

Liv smiled and tucked the notecard into the pocket of her robe. "Well, I guess hair and makeup it is."

After two hours of sitting in the hair and makeup chair, the receptionist walked into the salon and presented Liv with a large dress box. Inside was a black Lilly Pulitzer cocktail dress and silver-sequined wedges and, of course, another note: *Liv, you will always be my princess. See you at home! Love, Chase XOX.*

What is he up to? Liv thought as she held up the dress. "Am I going somewhere?" she asked. The spa staff shrugged their shoulders and giggled.

Liv went into the ladies locker room and changed into the dress and heels. Then she texted Chase. *Chase, what is going on?*

Chase texted back: *Are you wearing the dress?*

Yes.

Great. I'll see you soon!

But where?

At home, silly. XO.

Liv got into her car and began to drive home. *Why on earth am I all dressed up to go home?* As Liv drove down Seaspray Avenue, she noticed Christmas lights in the distance. When she pulled into her driveway, she could hardly believe her eyes. Her entire yard was covered in Christmas lights. Every palm tree, bush, and hedge was twinkling with lights. And in the middle of the yard was a sparkling Cinderella's carriage. Chase walked out of the front door wearing a tux and holding a single red rose. Liv's eyes began to fill with tears.

"Chase, I don't know what to say. No one has ever done anything like this for me before."

"C'mon. You ain't seen nothing yet," Chase said with a grin. He extended his arm and Liv wrapped her arm around his as he led her around the side yard and then into the backyard. Liv was dumbfounded by what she saw. A bougainvillea canopy covered in white string lights was set up next to the pool. Under the canopy was a perfectly set table for two. The sound of Frank Sinatra filled the air as Chase pulled out Liv's chair for her. He then handed Liv a dinner menu. Across the top it read, "Chase and Liv's Christmas Dinner, 2015." The dinner menu for the evening was the following:

Antipasto

Cocktail di Gamberi

Clams Casino

Insalata

Insalata Caprese
Insalata di Cesare
Entrées
Capellini Marinara with Shrimp
Chicken Parmesan
Dessert
Dancing under the stars,
followed by an evening of lovemaking

Liv looked around in amazement. "Chase, you recreated Renato's in my backyard?!"

"Yes, I believe I did, Liv." Chase stood up, lit the firepit, and then opened the champagne.

"Chase, I honestly don't know what to say. It's beautiful. No, it's breathtaking. I'm sorry…I think for the first time in my life, I'm actually at a loss for words."

Chase smiled and raised his glass. "Cheers to us, Liv, and to a lifetime of magical surprises."

And what a magical evening it was.

Christmas Day finally **arrived** and Liv was bound and determined to make this the best Christmas ever for her children. So, she had decided to hire Silver Sac Caterers to host an open house at her home from six to midnight.

At 6:00 p.m., Liv walked down the main staircase dressed in a stunning red satin cocktail dress with Rose trailing behind her in a black velvet dress with a red satin bow. Liv's home was, of course, decorated from top to bottom. The caterers had set up small round tables throughout her home and out by the pool. The tables were all covered in ivory tablecloths with miniature Christmas trees accenting each table. In the dining room was a grand buffet for the guests to enjoy—shrimp cocktail, Caesar salad, sliced tenderloin, baby roasted potatoes, and grilled mixed vegetables. Two open bars were also set up, one in the formal living room and the other out by the pool. And a beautiful dessert tower had been carefully assembled in the family room next to the Christmas tree.

Liv made her way out to the backyard where she spotted her three handsome sons sipping on martinis in their black tuxes with red tartan plaid bowties and matching cummerbunds. She went over and hugged each one.

"Merry Christmas, Mom," William said.

"Merry Christmas," said Liv. "I hope you're all having fun."

"Mom, this is a great party," said Austin. "And you really did go all out this year. I mean, even the outdoor Christmas lights are over the top."

Liv took a sip of her champagne and thought back to her evening with Chase in the backyard.

"Boys, Christmas is a time for magical moments," she said. "And please don't ever forget that. Now, listen, I want you all to have fun tonight, but keep your Christmas cheer down to a minimum, if you know what I mean."

William rolled his eyes and said, "Mom, you worry too much."

"It comes with the territory, son," Liv said as she walked away.

As soon as she entered the house, she spotted Chase standing by the Christmas tree, wearing a black tux. Liv made her way over to him.

"Merry Christmas, Liv," he said, as he gave her a hug.

"Merry Christmas, Chase. I'm so glad you're here."

"Liv, I must say this is some open house. So how many guests did you end up inviting?"

"Oh, only 200 of our closest friends and family. But between you and me, I never expected them all to show."

"Well, as usual, you've gone above and beyond."

"Chase, thanks again for the other night. I honestly can't stop thinking about it."

Chase leaned over and whispered in her ear, "Well, I can't stop thinking about you. Do you think I could steal you away to your bedroom for a minute?"

"Chase! There are 200 people in my house. There's no way we can do that right now."

"Liv, get your mind out of the gutter," Chase laughed. "I just wanted to give you your Christmas present."

"Oh, okay. And I have a little something for you as well."

Chase and Liv walked through the kitchen and then headed up the back staircase.

Liv closed her bedroom door behind them and locked it. Chase reached into his coat pocket and pulled out a long white box tied up with a red bow.

"Open it," he said, handing it to her.

Liv carefully untied the bow and opened the box. On a black velvet pillow sat a platinum necklace with a sideways cross that was covered in diamonds. "Chase, it's beautiful!"

"Here, let me help you put it on. I had it made for you down at Private Jewelers in Delray. I figured you could use an upgrade from the one I gave you at Sea Island."

"Chase I love it. I'm never taking it off." She hugged and kissed him. "Now let me go and get your gift." Liv went into her closet and returned with a Tiffany bag.

"Liv, what did you do?"

"You'll see, handsome. Just open it," she said, handing him the gift bag.

Chase sat the bag down on Liv's bed and pulled out a large Tiffany gift box, which was tied up with a red satin bow. He slid off the bow and opened the box. Inside was a Tiffany & Co. Atlas watch in platinum with a slate blue face.

"Turn it over," Liv said.

On the back of the watch was an engraving, *12-25-2015. XO.*

"Liv, I don't know what to say. I love it! Thank you."

"Thank you, Chase, for loving me, supporting me, and for sharing this unforgettable Christmas with me."

"Well, Liv, I can promise you this. We have many more Christmases in our future."

Liv gave him a huge kiss and prayed he was right.

CHAPTER 34

Would He Walk Out of Her Life Forever?

March, 2016. Unfortunately, at this point in time, Liv and Chase's relationship had remained a long-distance one due to the fact that Chase's coworker's wife had to undergo a double mastectomy. So, ever since New Year's Eve, Chase and Liv had been taking turns visiting each other. One month, Chase would fly down to Palm Beach and the next month, Liv would fly up to Atlanta.

On Friday, March 18th, Chase had flown down to Palm Beach for the weekend. Jeffrey was out of town once again with his traveling basketball team, and Rose was with Kurt for the weekend. So, Liv and Chase had decided to have a nice quiet weekend at home.

On Saturday, after an incredible night of lovemaking and a lazy morning around the house, Chase and Liv drove down to the Woolbright Farmers Market to pick up some fresh produce and a key lime pie from the Upper Crust bakery. On the way home, they stopped off at Fresh Market to purchase all of the ingredients they would need to prepare that night's dinner. Chase would be making his yummy chicken cilantro and Liv had decided to whip up a batch of her mother's world-famous scalloped potatoes.

When they arrived back home, Chase popped the trunk to Liv's Porsche Cayenne SUV and they both began taking the groceries into the house. As Liv was putting the groceries away, Chase said, "I'll go out and grab the rest." When he reached into the trunk, he suddenly heard a loud car engine idling behind him.

He turned around and there was Kurt, sitting behind the wheel of a black Hummer that was wrapped in his company's logo, Eagle Armor. Kurt quickly backed up, turned the SUV around, and rolled down his window.

"Now you listen to me, you little shit," Kurt seethed, "because I'm only going to say this once. I want you to stay away from my wife and daughter. Also, it would be in your best interest to stay up in Atlanta, because if you don't, you're putting you and your entire family in danger. Do you understand me?"

Chase nodded his head as Kurt slowly backed out of the driveway. Liv ran out of the house and wrapped her arms around Chase.

"Are you all right? You're shaking."

Chase put his arms around her and said, "Yes, Liv, but that's one scary dude."

"I know. What on earth was he doing here?"

"He came here to tell me to stay away from you."

"What?"

"Liv, he threatened me."

"Chase, we need to call the police so I can get another restraining order issued against him."

"No, Liv, just let it go."

"Are you sure?"

"Yes. Liv, I hate to say this, but a restraining order means nothing to that man."

Liv couldn't argue. She knew in her heart that Kurt was never going to leave her alone. Now the question in Liv's mind was, would Chase walk out of her life forever?

CHAPTER 35

Until There's a Ring

May 2016. Praise be to God! Chase had finally moved back to Palm Beach and thankfully he was still right by Liv's side. "Liv, Did you really think I would let that bully of an ex-husband of yours scare me off?" he had said. "I told you a long time ago that I wasn't going anywhere. And I always keep my promises." The first night Chase had returned to the island, he and Liv went over to Renato's for a romantic dinner followed by hours of lovemaking.

During the past few months, Liv and Chase had had numerous discussions about how and when to tell their families about their relationship. The problem for Liv was that Chase was thirty-one. He was exactly ten years older than Liv's sons and ten years younger than she was. So at this point, Liv now realized that her sons viewed Chase more as a peer and a friend than as a suitable partner for her.

And as far as Chase's family went, his mother was constantly trying to set him up on blind dates. Chase's mother wanted a grandchild desperately and his father wanted an heir to carry on the Montgomery family name. So, for months, Chase had been avoiding his mother's matchmaking skills until one day when she cornered him in the kitchen for a heart-to-heart talk.

"Chase, you know that I have always loved you and I always will. But there are some things in life you can't change about a person no matter how hard you try. I mean, Chase, just look at your Aunt Bonnie. For years, my parents tried to find her a husband until one day she finally confessed that she preferred women over men. And, Chase, as you know, I've exhausted all of my connections in trying to find you the perfect wife over these past few months. But at this point, I'm beginning to realize that you might be heading down the same road as your Aunt Bonnie, if you know what I mean. So Chase, please tell me the truth: Is this the case?"

Chase started to laugh so hard that he almost fell out of his chair. "No, mother, I can assure you that I'm one hundred percent not gay. Also, I'm more than capable of finding my own wife, thank you very much."

"But Chase, you haven't had a serious girlfriend since college. And let's face it, you always have been a little obsessed with Broadway musicals."

Chase began to laugh hysterically once again. "Mother, you're too much. I have to be heading off to work now, but please put your mind to rest. One day, mother, I'm going to be married to the most beautiful loving woman on the planet and we're going to have a house full of children. That much I can assure you."

So, as you can see, although almost a whole year had gone by, Liv and Chase were still in their same dilemma. Finally, one day Liv felt it was time to air her concerns to Chase.

"Chase," she said, "ever since Christmas, all I've done is think about how and when to tell our families about us. Now, before you say anything, please hear me out. My sons think of you as a friend, and Austin views you as an older brother. There is no way my three boys are going to be happy about our relationship. And another thing, I don't think

201

your family would be thrilled to learn about us being together, either. Unfortunately, over the past few years, your mother has been nothing but cold to me and downright rude at times. So, Chase, let's face it, there's no way she would be happy to learn that I'm sleeping with her golden child. And one more thing: this last year with you has been like a dream, but, Chase, a year really isn't long enough to truly get to know someone. Don't you agree?"

"Okay, Liv, so what are you trying to say?" asked Chase.

"What I'm saying is that for the sake of our families, and until we're really sure, and I mean *really* sure—I'm talking about an engagement ring on my finger and a wedding date on the calendar—I want to continue to keep our relationship a secret."

Chase paced the room for a few minutes and then finally said, "Okay, Liv. If this is what you think is best, I'm on board as long as you're still in my life."

"Handsome, I can assure you that I'm not going anywhere."

So it was settled. Liv and Chase's love affair would remain a secret. Or would it?

CHAPTER 36

Our Secret Is Safe

June, 2016. Liv was thrilled to have all of her children back under her roof. William and Austin had returned home for the summer and all three of Liv's sons were once again working at The Breakers Hotel.

On the morning of June 10th, Liv was racing out the door to get over to the Second Annual Olivia Donovan Golf Event for POTS Research. Thankfully, the event was sold out and was quite a bit larger than the previous year. This had a lot to do with Liv's new VP for her foundation. Kurt had been the original VP, so after their divorce became final, Liv began to search for a replacement. Much to her surprise, Chase immediately volunteered. Chase had helped with every aspect of this year's event, from ticket sales to getting sponsors and even securing silent auction items. Liv loved how well they worked together and she also admired how passionate he was about the foundation.

When Liv arrived at The Breakers golf course, the golfers were beginning to arrive and Chase was busy at the registration table checking them in and handing out gift bags. Liv went upstairs to check on the dining room set up for that evening. The ballroom looked beautiful, and Chase had even arranged for a live band this year. Liv took out her phone and sent Chase a text. *Chase, can you please come upstairs, I need your help with place cards.*

He quickly responded. *Sure, I'll be right there.*

Chase walked into the banquet room and said, "Liv, I gave you the table seating chart yesterday, but don't worry, I have an extra copy. So where are the place cards anyways?"

Liv picked up a small gift bag off of one of the tables and handed it to Chase. "I think they're in here."

Chase reached into the bag and pulled out a long black box that was tied up with a white satin bow.

"Liv, what is this?"

"Just open it, silly."

Chase carefully slipped off the bow and opened the box. On a black velvet pillow sat a platinum Italian Figaro chain with a solid platinum crucifix pendant.

"Liv, I love it! It's beautiful."

"Here, let me help you put it on." Liv carefully put the necklace around Chase's neck and then gave him a slow, passionate kiss. She then took his hand and said, "Chase, I want you to know that I couldn't have done this year's event without your help. Also, Chase, I truly do believe that God has brought us together and I will always be grateful for every day I've spent with you over this last year."

"Well, Liv," replied Chase, "I hope you know I feel exactly the same way. And, believe me, I'm never taking this off." Chase took Liv into his arms and began kissing her very softly.

Just then, Sally, the event planner walked into the banquet room. "Oh my gosh, I'm so sorry," she said. "I didn't realize anyone was in here." Her face turned three different shades of red. "I just...I mean, I just came up to check on the silent auction table," she continued, stumbling over her words.

Chase and Liv looked at each other unsure of what to say. Finally, Chase said, "Sally, I think everything is all taken care of up here for tonight, so you can go back down to the registration table."

"Oh, yes, of course," said Sally. "I didn't mean to interrupt." With that, Sally quickly turned and walked out of the banquet room.

"Oh, Chase, I'm so sorry." said Liv. "We've been so careful."

"Don't worry, Liv. I'll have a word with her, and I can assure you that our secret will remain safe."

But Liv couldn't help wondering, *Will it?*

CHAPTER 37

"A Place in My Heart"

June 6th, 2016. Once again, Liv was in a caravan of cars heading back up to Sea Island, Georgia. The cast of characters was the same as the year before with one exception. Chase had decided to stay behind.

As the cars drove over the Sidney Lanier Bridge and Liv's sons broke out in their traditional Sea Island song, Liv thought back to the conversation with Chase that had occurred a few weeks prior to the trip.

"Chase, I can't believe you're not coming to Sea Island with all of us," Liv had said.

"Listen, Liv, let's face it," Chase had replied, "we got lucky last year. But I can assure you that if I come along this year, we're going to get caught. Liv, the bottom line is this: It's just too hard for me to hide my feelings for you anymore."

"But, Chase, I really don't want to go back there without you. And don't you want to see your grandparents?"

"Of course I do, but they're planning on coming down here this year for the Fourth of July. Liv, you need to trust me on this. It's just not a good idea. And while we're on the subject of summer vacations, I guess I should tell you that I've also decided not to go to Jersey with you."

"What?! Are you kidding me? So, this is it—we're not going to go on vacations together anymore?"

"Liv, I never said that. What I am saying is I don't feel comfortable going on *family* vacations at this point. Besides, you and I can plan as many romantic getaways as you want, but the family vacations are over until we decide to tell everyone how we feel about each other. And Liv, you may not like this, but you know I'm right."

As much as Liv hated to admit it, she knew in her heart that Chase was, indeed, right. So now, here she was traveling back to Sea Island with Beau and her children, but without the love of her life.

The week had progressed the same as last year's vacation. There was the first-night room service dinner. Shrimp and grits over at Halyard's, fun-filled days on the beach, Liv's long morning beach walks, takeout from the Frederica House, group pictures on the lawn at The Lodge, followed by dinner at Colt & Alison's.

Beau and Liv even went back to the spa for another couple's massage. And at the conclusion of their massages, Beau opened a bottle of champagne. Liv lay in Beau's arms on an overstuffed chaise lounge as the afternoon sun streamed through the spa's stained-glass windows. She looked up at Beau and said, "You know I love you, right?"

"I know you do," said Beau. "And I love you too."

She snuggled her head against his chest and took another sip of her champagne. "And, Beau, I want you to know that I've thought about it. It's just—"

"It's just Chase."

Liv nodded. "I'm sorry, Beau."

"Love, there's no need to be sorry. And don't worry, Love, I promise you that I'm not going anywhere."

Liv interlocked her hand with Beau's and kissed it. "Promise?"

He kissed her hand and then her cheek. "Yes, Love, I promise."

Liv realized in this moment that love truly does come in many forms, and Beau Walker would forever have a piece of her heart and a place in her life.

CHAPTER 38

Liv's Dilemma

July 11th, 2016. Liv, Beau, and the children had all traveled back up to the Jersey Shore for their annual summer vacation. But unfortunately, Chase hadn't changed his mind about joining them. "Liv, my mind is made up when it comes to family vacations," he had told Liv.

"But Chase, I really want you to reconsider," said Liv. "It's very important to me that my family likes you and gets to know you better."

"Look, Liv, we'll have plenty of time for all of that, but believe me, now is definitely not the time."

"Okay, Chase, have it your way, but I don't want to hear you say one more word about Beau coming along on this trip because just like Sea Island, you've been invited." This was the first disagreement Liv and Chase had had in over a year of dating.

The first week at the Jersey Shore had started out just like the previous year. On the first night, the family gathered in the screened-in gazebo for a Lenny's Italian takeout dinner. Every morning, Liv took long walks on the beach, and, in keeping with tradition, her mother once again prepared a delicious lobster dinner, with David Santoro in attendance, of course. Liv, Beau, and Rose had also returned to the Wharfside Restaurant for a lovely seafood lunch overlooking the Manasquan Inlet, followed by a trip to the Point Pleasant Beach boardwalk. And this year, Liv's father had treated the guys to a day of golf over at the Manasquan River Country Club. Liv was thrilled to be back home and was enjoying every second with her family.

The morning of July 14th, Liv was in the kitchen pouring her morning coffee when the house phone rang. She answered and was pleasantly surprised to hear her Uncle Rollins's voice.

"Good morning, Liv, and welcome home," said her uncle.

"Thanks, Unc. It's great to be back."

"I spoke to your mother the other day and she said you were all enjoying yourselves."

"Oh, yes. It's been a great week so far. And the weather's been perfect."

"Well, let's just hope it holds up for the family barbecue that your mother has planned for all of us on Sunday."

"Unc, we both know that my father is in charge of the barbecue on Sunday." They both laughed.

Then Uncle Rollins said, "Liv, I'm sending Kevin to come and pick you up tomorrow morning at ten to bring you up to our Westfield office."

"Oh? Okay. Is everything all right?"

"Of course, Liv. Everything's fine. I just need to speak to you about a little family business, that's all. So I'll see you tomorrow then?"

"Yes, Unc. I'll see you tomorrow."

Liv hung up the phone wondering what this meeting could possibly be about. The next morning, she walked into her uncle's office wearing her pink and white plaid St. John's dress suit and her Tiffany cultured pearl necklace. Uncle Rollins immediately rose out of his chair behind his massive mahogany desk to greet her.

"Oh, Liv, it's so nice to have you home," he said, giving her a warm embrace.

"Thanks, Unc."

"Now, please have a seat."

Liv took a seat and nervously put down her handbag.

"So, Liv, you must be wondering why I wanted to see you today."

Liv nodded.

"Well, as you know, the Gallagher family has a strict policy about keeping business matters and family matters separate. That's one of the reasons we've been in business for over 160 years. With that being said, I have some things that you and I really need to discuss."

"Okay," Liv said quietly.

"Liv, this whole family loves you, and what Kurt has put you through has been a complete nightmare. But unfortunately, Olivia, we do have a rather big issue on our hands. After Kurt's sudden and unexpected departure, the family came together to bail you out financially."

"Oh, Unc, I know, and I will forever be grateful for everything that the family has done for me and my children."

"Olivia, this is extremely difficult for me to say especially with my track record in the love department." Uncle Rollins was currently on his fifth wife. "But Palm Beach is a very small town," he continued. "And to say that your romance with this much younger man has been the talk of the town would be a huge understatement. And to make matters even worse, the last time I was down in Palm Beach, I happened to go over to Ta-boo for lunch. And much to my surprise, what did I see? You and Chase sitting in a booth next to the fireplace making out in the middle of the day like a couple of teenagers!"

Oh, God, Liv thought. She looked around the room unsure of how to respond.

211

"Liv, the bottom line is this: the Gallagher family name cannot be tarnished by this seedy love affair of yours. I just can't have it. So here's where I'm at in regards to your situation. It ends, Olivia. Immediately. And if it doesn't, the Gallagher's financial help stops now. Do you understand what that would mean for you and your family? Olivia, you would be forced to sell your home. Austin and William would have to drop out of Duke at once! Also, There would be no more private school for Jeffrey and Rose, and your $25,000 a month allowance would end today.

"Now, Olivia, this family is more than happy to support your very luxurious lifestyle, but if you continue to see Chase Montgomery, you are going to find yourself shit out of luck in the financial department. Also, Olivia, you're a beautiful woman and I know you will have no problem finding a suitable partner, and one that the family will welcome with open arms. So Olivia, have I made my position clear here today?"

Liv's head was spinning. Finally, she said, "Unc, so you're basically asking me to choose between the man I love and financial security. Is that correct?"

"Yes, Olivia. It's quite simple. Stop seeing Chase Montgomery or you're cut off. Now, I'm late for my lunch meeting so I really must be heading out."

Uncle Rollins stood up and buttoned his suit coat.

"Have a safe ride back down to the shore and I'll see you on Sunday. And Olivia, I know you'll make the right decision." With that, he strode out of the office.

When Liv got into her car, she immediately called her Aunt Betty. "Auntie, you're never going to believe what happened in my meeting with Uncle Rollins!"

"Oh, boy," sighed Aunt Betty, "what did my dear sweet brother have to say to you?"

Liv quickly recapped her conversation with her uncle.

"Okay Liv, just take a deep breath," said Aunt Betty, "and tell Kevin to drop you off at my house. The guys won't be back from their day of fishing until later this afternoon and your mother has taken Rose over to the yacht club for the day. I'll run up to the Normandy Market and grab us some lunch and a bottle of wine. But don't worry, Liv. I promise you we'll get this whole mess sorted out."

"Okay, Auntie, if you say so."

"Liv, I got this."

As soon as Liv walked into Aunt Betty's house, Auntie gave her a big hug and handed her a huge glass of wine.

"Livvy, I stopped by your parents' house after I picked up our lunch and I got your bathing suit. Why don't you go change in the guest house and I'll meet you out by the pool?"

"Okay, Auntie, and thank you."

Liv and Aunt Betty sat side by side in two white wooden rocking chairs that overlooked the pool and Barnegat Bay.

"Thanks for getting lunch, Auntie," said Liv.

"No worries, Livvy. You know I'm always here for you." Auntie reached over and squeezed Liv's hand. "Well, kid, this is quite a mess you've gotten yourself into now, isn't it? And Liv, I told you a year ago that this was going to be a bumpy ride, didn't I?"

"Yes, Auntie, and you were right as usual. But now what? And just so you know, I honestly don't care about the money. Auntie, Don't you remember when Kurt and I first got married? We had nothing. We were eating out of our vegetable garden, for God's sake."

"Yes, Liv, I remember, but times are different now and you have to think about your children. Do you really want Austin and William to be forced to drop out of Duke? And I know Rose would be happy in a public school, but what about Jeffrey? High school is such a difficult time for any teenager and he's already been through so much. And, Liv, are you really willing to give up your home?"

"So, Auntie, basically you're telling me to end it?"

Aunt Betty took a big sip of wine. "Yes, Liv. I think you should. But, for better or worse, I know that your heart always leads you, not your head."

"Ain't that the truth?" Liv said as she took another sip of wine.

"Well, Livvy, let's face it, you're never going to stop seeing him, so we're just going to have to come up with another solution."

"Like what?"

"Well, to start with, you're going to have to be a lot more discreet. No more parading around town with him. And when you do go anywhere, you must always pay in cash. Olivia, I'm telling you, you must never leave a paper trail. Do you understand me?"

"Yes, Auntie, but Chase has always been such a big part of Austin's life. So even if I broke up with him today, we would still see each other."

"Yes, and that's what you're going to explain to your sweet Uncle Rollins at the barbecue on Sunday. Tell him that you're willing to end your romantic relationship with Chase, but you still want to remain friends for Austin's sake. I would also throw in there that you've started to have some strong feelings for Beau."

"What?!"

"Look, Liv, Beau will be the perfect decoy. You have to start making everyone believe that Beau Walker is your new love interest. Trust me, Liv, it will definitely calm the waters."

"Okay," said Liv. "And then what?"

"Five years."

"What do you mean 'five years'?"

"You and Chase must keep your relationship under wraps for the next five years."

"What? And why five years?"

"Because, Livvy, in five years, Austin and William will have graduated from college. They'll be off on their own and out of your home. Hell, they might even be married by then, and Jeffrey's such a talented basketball player I'm sure he'll be getting a free ride to college. So that will just leave you and Rose at home. At that point, you can sell that huge home of yours and downsize if you want. And, Liv, if in five years you're still madly in love with Chase, I promise to go to bat for the two of you with the family. Also, Livvy, my dear sweet brother will be in his late seventies by then, and you see, Liv, people do tend to mellow with age. So, yes, Liv, I believe your best bet is the five-year plan."

Liv gazed out at the Barnegat Bay and finally said, "Okay, Auntie, I'll do it. I just hope Chase is on board."

"Liv, if he loves you as much as you say he does, he'll agree to it."

"Auntie, I really hope you're right."

Aunt Betty raised her wine glass. "Cheers to the five-year plan!"

As they clinked glasses, Liv wondered, *How am I ever going to explain this all to Chase?*

CHAPTER 39

The Five-Year Plan

Two weeks later, Liv was back in Palm Beach. She had decided that the best way to break the news to Chase about the five-year plan was over a romantic lunch at her home. She called over to the beach club and arranged to have two lobster rolls, truffle fries, and coleslaw delivered at noon. She then asked Ms. Dee to help her set up a lovely table for two in her bedroom's sitting area. She carefully laid out her great-grandmother's rosebud tablecloth, along with her pink Depression-era glass dishes and stemware. Next to the table in a silver ice bucket, she placed a bottle of Veuve Clicquot on ice. She stepped back to admire the table and thought to herself, *God, I hope this goes well.*

At 12:30, Chase walked through Liv's front door wearing his navy Brooks Brothers suit and looking as handsome as ever.

"So, Liv, why did you want to have lunch at the house today?" Chase asked. "We usually go over to Ta-boo on Fridays. And where is everyone, anyways?"

"Well, the boys are all at work, Rose is at summer camp, and Ms. Dee is out running errands. Come on, I have a little surprise for you upstairs," Liv said as she took Chase's hand and led him up the main staircase to her bedroom.

"Wow, Liv, what's all this?" Chase said when he saw the lunch setup.

"I just thought it would be nice to have lunch up here today. And also, I don't want us to be interrupted."

"Well, Liv, I like the way you think," Chase said as he leaned over and gave her a romantic kiss.

"Look," said Liv, "I had all of your favorites delivered from the beach club."

Liv pulled out Chase's chair for him and then she poured them each a glass of champagne.

"Cheers to romantic afternoons," Liv said. They touched glasses and began to enjoy their delicious lunch. "So how's work going today?" Liv asked.

"It's good so far," said Chase. "I'm just glad it's Friday. So I was thinking, maybe tomorrow we could spend the day over at the beach club. I heard it's supposed to be a beautiful weekend and I thought we could take the sailboat out."

Liv put her fork down and then reached across the table to hold Chase's hand.

"Chase, We need to talk about my Jersey trip," she said.

"Okay, but when I spoke to Austin yesterday, he told me that you all had a great time up there. And please don't worry, I'm not going to bring up the whole Beau situation anymore. I've decided to just let that all go."

"Chase, something happened in New Jersey."

"Okay. So, what happened?" Chase asked as he took a big bite out of his lobster roll.

Liv nervously recapped the conversation she'd had with her Uncle Rollins. Chase stood up and threw his napkin down on his chair. He then began to pace the room.

"Liv, is this some kind of joke? You do realize this is blackmail, don't you? And this coming from a man who is on—I'm sorry, how many wives has he had again?"

"Five."

"Right, and his current wife is younger than you, I believe. Correct?"

"Yes, she is."

"So, Liv, if you were a man and you were in a relationship with a younger woman, your family wouldn't have an issue with that?"

"Yes, Chase, I know. And I do understand that this situation is completely unfair, but I'm telling you, Uncle Rollins isn't going to change his mind and he means business. But don't worry. Aunt Betty has come up with a plan for us."

"Well, this should be good. Okay, so what is Aunt Betty's clever plan?"

Liv summarized her conversation with Aunt Betty.

"So let me get this straight. You expect us to keep our relationship a secret for the next five years?!" asked Chase. "Liv, We're not talking about five months. We're talking about five *years*."

"Look, Chase, I realize it's a lot to ask, but it really is the only way. I can't risk forcing my children to leave their current schools. And Chase, I fought so hard to keep this home for them. If we don't do this, their entire worlds are going to be turned upside down, and I just can't do that to them."

Chase unbuttoned his top collar button, loosened his tie, and took a seat on the edge of Liv's bed. Liv sat beside him and took his hand.

"Five years?" Chase asked.

"Yes, Chase, it's the only way."

"Well, Liv, I have to be honest with you. I was willing to keep our relationship under wraps for a little while longer, but five years is just too much to ask. And I do realize that I might be getting a little ahead of myself, but on a different topic, I really did envision us starting a family someday."

Chase then bowed his head as he sat silently on the bed. Liv put her arm around Chase and placed her head on his shoulder.

"Chase, I have been very fortunate to have been blessed with four beautiful children, and when you're in a relationship with someone who is much younger than you are, of course the issue of having children will eventually come up one day. Chase, I guess what I'm trying to say is, I love you, and when you love someone, you want to give them everything that their heart desires. So how about this: What if, after the first of the year, I promise to freeze my eggs? Would that relieve some of the pressure of us having a baby some day?"

"You would do that?" Chase asked.

"Chase Montgomery, I would do absolutely anything for you." She then softly kissed him on his cheek.

"Okay," he sighed. "So I guess this beautiful relationship of ours will just have to continue to be a secret."

"Thank you, Chase."

And for the rest of the afternoon, tangled up under her sheets, Liv showed her gratitude to Chase over and over again.

CHAPTER 40

Our Cottage by the Sea

September, 2016. Liv and Chase had officially decided to put their five-year plan into action. And because of this, Chase moved out of his parents' guest house and into a charming two-bedroom, two-bath cottage at 1022 Nassau Street in Delray Beach. The 1938 white beach cottage with blue shutters was now Liv and Chase's secret love nest. There were gorgeous pine floors throughout, an updated kitchen, and a beautiful, artistic wood beam vaulted ceiling in the living room and master bedroom. The cottage also had a rustic stone chimney and a lovely cobblestone patio in the back yard that was surrounded by lush, tropical plants.

The home was located just two blocks from the ocean, and was also in walking distance to the very popular Atlantic Avenue. Although the cottage was only thirty-five minutes south of Liv's home, Chase and Liv felt as though they were a million miles away from the prying eyes of Palm Beach.

Also, Delray Beach had recently become a very desirable tourist destination, so Liv and Chase could easily blend right into the hustle and bustle of this fast-growing beach town. They enjoyed weekly dinners on Atlantic Avenue over at Cut 432, City Oyster, and Casa L'Acqua.

But The Grove was by far their favorite restaurant in Delray. The Grove was a five-star restaurant that was owned and operated by a young and talented chef named Michael Haycook. Michael took great pride in using only the freshest ingredients, and he also insisted that nothing be prepared ahead of time. To put it simply, a dinner at The Grove was truly a unique and memorable experience.

So for Liv, the last few months in Delray had been like a dream come true. At sunset, Chase and Liv would take long walks on the beach. Friday nights were spent dining on the Ave, and on Saturdays, they would take turns cooking for each other. Every Sunday morning, they'd walk down to the farmers' market in Old School Square to buy fresh produce, followed by brunch over at Luna Rosa. And on rainy afternoons, they would make love to the sound of raindrops dancing across the cottage's tin roof.

September 28th, 2016. Liv was busy in the kitchen preparing homemade lasagna, Caesar salad, and garlic bread for that evening's dinner. It was the perfect fall day in South Florida—low humidity, a crystal clear blue sky, with just a hint of autumn in the air. Liv put the lasagna in the oven and then went out back to set the table, which was now under a beautiful canopy of blooming bougainvillea. Meanwhile, Chase was in his office on an unexpected conference call for work. When he finished his call, he walked into the kitchen,

"Liv, it smells great in here. How much longer until dinner's ready?"

"I'd say in about forty-five minutes I'll have everything on the table."

"Great. I think I'll go for a quick run before dinner, if that's okay."

"Sure. So how was your conference call?"

"I'll tell you all about it over dinner," Chase replied as he hurried out the back door.

At seven o'clock, Liv and Chase sat down to enjoy dinner. The fire-pit in the backyard was glowing and the string lights that Chase had hung in the bougainvillea transformed their backyard into a dreamy atmosphere.

"I love it here, Chase," said Liv as she looked around the backyard. "You truly have made us the perfect home."

Chase took a bite of the lasagna and then a big sip of red wine. "Liv, we need to talk about my conference call today."

"Okay," Liv said as she put her fork down.

"Liv, as you know, I've been up for a promotion for some time now, and I found out today that I got it."

"Chase, that's wonderful news!"

"It is, but there is one small problem."

"Okay. What is it?"

"Liv, the job is up in Ponte Vedra."

"What? I don't understand."

"Liv, They offered me the vice president position in their Ponte Vedra office. Liv, this is a huge opportunity for me, and if I accept, I would actually be the youngest VP at Morgan in the country. They're also prepared to purchase a home up there for me, and to sweeten the deal, they even threw in a membership at the Ponte Vedra Lodge and Golf Club. Liv, you know I love Delray, but Ponte Vedra is five hours away and it would definitely help us with our five-year plan. So what do you think?"

Liv's head was spinning. "Chase, I honestly don't know what to say. I mean, I love our life here."

"I know you do," said Chase, "and so do I, but Liv, we have to be smart."

Liv looked nervously around their beautiful backyard and finally said, "I hate to say this, but I guess you're right. We can't risk anyone finding out about us. At least not yet anyways."

"So do you want me to take the job?"

"Chase, what I want is to stay in this beach cottage with you forever, but I know you taking this job is what's best for the both of us."

Liv's eyes began to fill with tears.

"Liv, please don't cry," said Chase. "It's all going to be fine. And don't worry, I'm definitely not giving up this house. I love it here, and I know we can make this work."

"Promise?"

"Yes, Liv, I promise."

Chase got up from the table and came around to give Liv a kiss.

And at that moment, Liv finally believed that Chase Montgomery IV would always keep every promise he ever made to her.

CHAPTER 41

Ponte Vedra

October 20th, 2016. Liv was on a plane heading up to Ponte Vedra to celebrate her birthday with Chase. Unfortunately, Liv had spent a lot of time in the past over at the Mayo Clinic when she was so very ill with POTS. But today, she was excited to return to Jacksonville, healthy and head over heels in love.

After a quick twenty-minute drive from the Jacksonville airport, Chase pulled up to his oceanfront, one-story, gray-shingled beach cottage. The home was darling with a turquoise front door and matching shutters. Under each of the front windows hung White window boxes that housed pink, white, and red geraniums—all of which were in full bloom.

"Chase, this house is a dream!" said Liv as she got out of the car.

"I thought you'd like it," Chase said as he popped the trunk and pulled out Liv's luggage. "Come on, I'll give you the grand tour."

As Liv stepped through the front door, she was immediately in awe of the ocean views. All along the back of the house were double French doors that looked out onto the ocean. The floors of the home were pine and there was white wainscoting throughout. In front of the white brick fireplace in the living room was a cozy gray sofa and a driftwood glass-top coffee table. When Liv walked into the kitchen, she immediately fell in love with its white glass-panel cabinets and cobalt blue granite countertops.

"Chase, I don't know what to say. It's everything I'd imagined and more."

"Come on, let me show you outside," said Chase. Liv stepped out onto the large wooden deck to find an intimate sitting area with a fire pit, a gas grill, and a rustic harvest dining table. On the edge of the deck sat blue and green planters that held more blooming geraniums.

"Chase, this house is perfect," Liv said.

"It really is, isn't it? Now I know it's small and they did offer me a much larger home over on the golf course, but there was no way I could turn down this view."

Chase took Liv back inside and showed her how he had converted the second bedroom into his home office.

"And last but not least..." he said, as he opened the door to the master bedroom. Liv entered to find a king-size bed with a white duvet cover that had been placed in front of another wood-burning fireplace. On the white duvet, red rose pedals spelled out "Happy Birthday." Chase walked across the room and opened the windows to let in the sound of the crashing surf. "Welcome home, Liv," he said, kissing her softly.

"So what did you plan for my birthday tonight, handsome?" Liv asked.

With a devilish grin, Chase replied, "Well, first, I'm going to spend the afternoon making love to you, and then I think we should take a long, hot bath. I've also arranged for the Ponte Vedra Lodge to set up a romantic dinner for the two of us out on the deck. Sound good?"

"Sounds perfect," Liv said as she kissed him again.

Chase slowly unzipped Liv's dress and watched as it dropped to the floor. He then stepped back.

"Chase, what are you doing?" Liv asked.

"I just want to look at your beautiful body for a moment."

Liv walked over to the rose-covered bed and lay down.

"I want you, Chase," she said as she began to touch herself. "Please make love to me, Chase. You have no idea how much I've missed you."

Chase quickly removed his clothes and lay down next to her. He slid his finger inside of her as she began to moan. "I want to feel you cum first" he said. "Cum for me, Liv."

"I will," she whispered. "I'll cum for you."

Hot liquid streamed down Chase's fingers and then he moved quickly on top of her. She wrapped her legs around him until she felt him explode inside of her. After, he rested his head on her breasts, while he was still inside of her. Her fingers made small circles up and down his back as she gently kissed his neck.

"Happy birthday, Liv," he whispered and soon, while listening to the sound of the waves crashing onto the shore, they both drifted off for a long afternoon nap.

Later that evening, out on the deck, sitting at the harvest table with the ocean and full moon as their backdrop, they dined on a lovely birthday dinner: oysters on the half-shell, Caesar salad, and surf and turf.

"Chase, this dinner and this day have been amazing," said Liv. "Thank you so very much."

"Well, Liv, I guess I'm starting to know what you like by now," Chase said with a smile.

Liv laughed. "You definitely do, handsome."

"Liv, I just love making you smile, and you know that."

"I do, Chase, and I appreciate everything you've done for me, not just today but every day," Liv said. "So tell me, how do you like it up here?"

Chase looked around. "Liv, what's not to like? My office is less than ten minutes down the road. And I told you they threw in the golf course and beach club membership. Also, the people up here are very friendly and it's so much more laid back than South Florida. Plus, I've been driving up to Sea Island every other weekend to check on my grandparents, as you know. So Liv, basically, life up here is perfect. Except for one thing."

Liv took a large sip of her Caymus select cab. "Me?" she asked.

"Yes, Liv. Now look, I understand why we're doing what we're doing, but I really do hope someday down the road, you, me, and Rose will be calling Ponte Vedra home."

"Chase, I honestly don't know what my future holds for me, but I definitely can't think of a future without you in it."

"I was hoping you'd say that." Chase stood up and lit the fire pit then, turning to go inside, he said, "I'll be right back." Shortly, he returned with a small Tiffany's gift bag and a cupcake with a lit candle. "Happy birthday, Liv," he said as he handed her the bag.

Liv blew out the candle as she made a wish, then she pulled out a small blue box from the gift bag that was tied up in a white satin bow. In the black velvet box sat a Tiffany Victoria platinum and diamond band.

"Chase, it's stunning, but you really shouldn't be doing all of this. I'm going to run out of fingers, silly," she said giggling.

Chase kissed Liv as he gently slid the ring on her finger. Then he kissed her hand and said, "Just wait, Liv, one day you're going to be my wife. You'll see."

Liv closed her eyes as he kissed her again and hoped her birthday wish one day would come true.

CHAPTER 42

New Year's Eve

December 31st, 2016. As Liv stood in her backyard releasing Chinese wishing lanterns up into the clear brisk winter sky, she couldn't help but reflect on the year's events. Austin and William were thriving at Duke, Jeffrey was a rising star on and off of the basketball court, and little Rose continued to bring joy into Liv's life on a daily basis.

Sadly, Kurt continued to be a troublesome thorn in Liv's side. He was constantly dragging her into family court over minor issues. He had also tried once again to get his hands on Liv's shares of Gallagher Construction, but fortunately, as Liv's attorney put it, Kurt didn't have a leg to stand on.

Chase and Liv continued to split their time between Delray Beach and Ponte Vedra. And this year, instead of exchanging Christmas presents, they had decided to sneak down to Miami for a romantic one-night getaway at the Mandarin Oriental. At the hotel, they enjoyed couples massages at the spa, sunset cocktails on the rooftop at Juvia, and dinner at Il Gabbiano.

And in less than a week, Liv was scheduled for her egg retrieval up at the Mayo Clinic in Jacksonville.

For Liv, she finally felt as though she had found the peace in her life that she had been searching for over the last few years. And on this New Year's Eve, as she watched the Chinese lanterns float away into the night sky, she did wonder what the year 2017 would bring her way.

CHAPTER 43

My Baby

January 6th, 2017. Liv was back up in Ponte Vedra for the weekend and couldn't wait for her egg retrieval on Monday. At this point, she was so hopped up on hormones that she just wanted the procedure to be over and done with.

But until then, Chase had planned a fun-filled weekend for the both of them. On Friday night, they went over to Sliders Oyster Bar in Neptune Beach, where they feasted on crostino with beef tenderloin, steamed and raw oysters, followed by shrimp and cheese grits. After dinner, they walked down the street and stumbled upon Pete's Bar. Pete's Bar had been around since 1933. It was a locals', cash-only, late-night hangout that provided beer, mixed drinks, and pool tables.

Liv stopped in front of the red neon Pete's Bar sign and said, "Come on, Chase. Let's go in."

"Liv, This doesn't look like your kind of place, if you know what I mean," Chase replied.

Liv reached down and grabbed Chase's hand, pulling him into the bar. Once inside the crowded, smoke-filled joint, Liv shouted, "Chase, why don't you go and get us a couple of beers while I grab us a pool table?"

Chase smiled and walked over to the bar. Liv found an empty pool table, and as she began racking the balls, two men approached.

"So, are you any good?" one of them asked.

"I can hold my own," Liv replied, chalking up a cue.

"Oh yeah? Well, I guess we'll see about that," the man said as he placed a hundred-dollar bill on the table.

"You've got yourself a game," said Liv just as Chase returned with the beers.

Into Liv's ear, Chase whispered, "Liv, do you even know how to play pool?"

"Don't worry, handsome. I got this."

And apparently, she did. Chase and Liv won the first game, then the second game. "Okay, this is the last game of the night. But let's make it really interesting," said the man as he placed $500 on the pool table.

Soon, a large crowd gathered around the table, watching as Liv sunk one ball after another. Chase was amazed and also couldn't stop smiling. Once again, Liv led them to victory. She picked up the $500 and said, "Nice doing business with you, gentlemen. Have a great rest of the night." She then grabbed Chase's hand and led him out of the bar.

Once outside, Liv quickly flagged down a cab and soon they were heading back to Chase's house. In the back of the cab, Chase laughed and said, "Well, Liv, I guess you really do know how to play pool after all."

Liv leaned over and kissed him. "Mr. Montgomery, you should know that there are very few things that I'm not very good at. And when we get back to your house, I'll be happy to show you a few more of my many talents."

Liv and Chase spent the rest of the night out on the deck in front of the fire pit, making love under a brisk starry sky.

On Saturday, Liv and Chase enjoyed a relaxing lunch over at the Ponte Vedra Lodge & Beach Club, and then spent the rest of the day on the beach. In the late afternoon, they strolled down the beach picking up sand dollars, sea glass, and whelk shells.

Just as Liv and Chase were about to turn around to head back to their beach chairs, Chase grabbed Liv's hand and said, "Come on, let's take a swim."

Holding hands, they ran into the warm water and dove under the surf. Once out past the shore break, Chase took Liv into his arms and gave her a salty, romantic kiss.

"I want you," he said as he pushed her bathing suit aside and slipped his finger inside of her.

"I want you too," said Liv, reaching down and slipping off her bathing suit. Chase removed his trunks and held Liv in his arms. She wrapped her legs around him as he slid inside of her. And there, in broad daylight, Chase made love to Liv in the sea.

On Sunday, Chase arranged for a couple's massage over at the Ponte Vedra Spa and lunch out by the spa's private pool. As they sat poolside, they dined on tomato, mozzarella, and basil flatbread pizzas, and enjoyed a bottle of Veuve Clicquot. After lunch, they swam under the pool's waterfall, and then it was time for their sixty-minute relaxation massages.

When the massages were over, the therapist said, "So, as you're both aware, you have an hour of alone-time in the suite. Please feel free to enjoy the steam room, hot tub, and this complimentary bottle of champagne."

"Thank you," Chase replied as the therapist left the room.

Chase stood up and walked over to Liv. He took her hand and led her into the steam room. He began kissing her and touching her breasts. She got down on her knees and began licking him. She slid her mouth slowly up and down, arousing him until he couldn't take it anymore. He then opened the steam room door and led her over to the hot tub. Once in the tub, he handed her a glass of champagne. She took a sip and then climbed on top of him. She moved slowly up and down, running her fingers through his jet-black hair. She leaned over and kissed his neck as he exploded inside of her. She lay her wet body on top of his and thought, *I've never been this happy in my entire life.*

Once back at the house, Chase fired up the grill to cook Liv a nice steak dinner. In the meantime, Liv decided to take a hot shower and put on some comfy clothes. As she stepped out of the shower, she wrapped herself in a large bath sheet. Suddenly, she felt a sharp pain in her abdomen. She then noticed drops of blood on the white tile floor.

A stream of blood began to run down her leg. She doubled over in excruciating pain as the room began to spin. She went to hold on to the bathroom vanity, but lost her grip and collapsed.

Fifteen minutes later, Chase walked into what looked like a scene straight out of a horror movie. Liv was unconscious, lying in a massive pool of blood. Chase ran over to check her pulse. It was slow and weak. He ripped the top sheet off of his bed and wrapped her up in it. Then he gently carried her to his car, placing her carefully in the backseat.

The Mayo Clinic was only ten minutes away and Chase knew that it was Liv's best chance. "Hold on, Liv!" he said as he sped out of his driveway. In less than ten minutes, he pulled up to the emergency room entrance at the Mayo Clinic, jumped out of the car, and rushed into the ER. He then grabbed the first emergency room attendant that he saw, and soon, Liv was on a stretcher being wheeled back to emergency.

The nurse at the reception desk began asking Chase a series of questions. Finally, out of frustration, Chase said, "Look, she's been a patient at Mayo for years now and I'm sure that you have all of her medical records on file. Also, she's scheduled to have an egg retrieval procedure tomorrow morning at 8:00 a.m. with Dr. Conlen."

"Okay, sir," said the nurse. "Let me page Dr. Conlen and we'll go from there."

Chase nodded with tears in his eyes and then took a seat in the waiting room. With his head in his hands, he began to pray. *Please, dear God, please let her be okay. She just has to be okay.*

Dr. Conlen soon entered the waiting room. "Chase?"

"Dr. Conlen! Is she okay?"

"Yes, Chase, thanks to your quick thinking, but she's lost a lot of blood and she's going to need emergency surgery."

"Okay Dr. Conlen, but what the hell happened?"

"Chase, she had a miscarriage."

"What?! She was pregnant?"

"Yes. Only six or seven weeks by my estimation, but unfortunately, it was an ectopic pregnancy that had ruptured. So I'm going to have to perform laparoscopic surgery to remove the ectopic pregnancy and also her fallopian tubes. Chase, I'm sorry, but I have no choice."

"Dr. Conlen, just tell me: What's the bottom line?"

"Unfortunately, Chase, the bottom line is this: there will be no more children in Olivia's future."

"But what about the egg retrieval?"

"Chase, It's far too late for that, I'm afraid. Just be grateful she's alive because I'm telling you, you almost lost her today."

Chase nodded as tears began to roll down his face.

"Now, I suggest you go back to your house and get some of her things," Dr. Conlen continued. "She's going to have to stay in the hospital for at least forty-eight hours after the surgery. But don't worry, I've requested a private room for her and you're more than welcome to stay with her if you'd like." Dr. Conlen reached out and touched

Chase's arm. "I have to get her into surgery now, but I promise to give you a call when the procedure is over." Dr. Conlen then turned and went back through the emergency room doors.

Chase stood numb and frozen in the waiting room. *She was pregnant*, he thought. *The woman of my dreams was pregnant with my baby. But not anymore. And she never will be again.*

Epilogue

Liv and Chase were now driving back down to Palm Beach after Liv had rested for over a week at Chase's home under his loving care. Chase had been wonderful in every way: he'd helped Liv bathe, dress, and he even made her homemade chicken noodle soup. But, unfortunately, Liv could hardly even look at him. Every time she tried, tears would start to roll down her face. She desperately wanted to thank him for taking such good care of her, but she had barely said two words to him since she'd been discharged from the hospital.

Finally, after a long, five-hour drive, they pulled into Liv's driveway. Chase carefully helped Liv out of the car and then grabbed the luggage out of the trunk.

Ms. Dee immediately came out of the house to greet them.

"Welcome home, Ms. Olivia," she said as she gave Liv a gentle hug. "You gave us all quite a scare up there." Liv nodded. Ms. Dee continued, "Now, I know the doctor said no stairs for another week, so I have the downstairs guest room all ready for you."

"Thank you," Liv replied quietly as they all stepped inside. "Ms. Dee, the family still doesn't know anything, right?"

"Of course not, Ms. Olivia. They all think you went up to the Mayo Clinic for your annual checkup and ended up catching the flu. And as you know, Rose is with Mr. Kurt until Tuesday, and Jeffrey went down to the Keys for the weekend. So you'll have all weekend to rest in peace."

Ms. Dee and Chase quickly got Liv settled into the downstairs guestroom. "I'll go and make you something to eat," said Ms. Dee as she left the room.

Chase sat down on the side of the bed and took Liv's hand. "Liv, you're going to be just fine. You know that, right?" Liv nodded as she fought back the tears. "And Liv, I really wish I could stay the night, but since I took last week off, I have to be back in the office first thing tomorrow morning."

"I know, Chase, and thanks for taking such good care of me."

Chase leaned over and gave her a gentle kiss. "Now, please try to get some rest and I'll give you a call in a couple of hours to check on you, okay?"

"Okay, Chase. And please drive safe."

"Don't worry, I will," he said as he walked out of the room.

Liv turned over on her side as the tears began to fall onto her pillow. Ms. Dee soon appeared with a dinner tray of chicken noodle soup and a chicken salad sandwich on rye.

"Let it out, Ms. Olivia," she said as she carefully placed the tray on the end of the bed.

Liv began to sob uncontrollably. Ms. Dee gently embraced her and said, "It's all going to be all right, Ms. Olivia. I promise."

"No! No, Ms. Dee, it's *not* all going to be all right! Don't you understand? He's going to leave me! I lost our baby! I lost our baby!" It was the first time Liv had said those words out loud. "And this last year has all been too much, Ms. Dee. Trying to keep our relationship a secret, and now I can't give him the one thing that he wants most in the world. So, no, Ms. Dee, I know this relationship is over! He's just too sweet and kind to tell me, but mark my words, he will leave me."

Ms. Dee held both of Liv's hands and said, "Ms. Olivia, we don't know that yet. All we know is that the good Lord has brought you back home safe and sound. And you listen to me, Ms. Olivia. Your children need you, so you let the tears fall as much as you want over the weekend, but on Monday, you're going to have to pull yourself together for their sake. And as far as Mr. Chase goes, we'll just have to wait and see where his heart leads him. But I have a strong feeling that his heart is going to lead him right back here to you."

Liv hugged Ms. Dee tightly and prayed that she was right.

To be continued…

…in Samantha Dupree's forthcoming novel,
Live, Love, Be…

Acknowledgments

Once again, I would like to thank my four beautiful children for loving and supporting me, and for allowing their mother to explore her passion for writing.

I would also like to thank my father, Peter, who is hands down my biggest fan! To watch you read my first novel and sign endless copies for our family and friends was truly priceless. And yes, Dad, somehow your little girl has become an author. I love you, Dad. XO

And to the man who has held my hand so tight and has refused to let go. You are the true definition of a soulmate. Thank you for loving me through the good, the bad, and the in-between. And as you already know, you will have a place in my heart forever. XOXO

And last but not least to all of my readers…there are times in your life when God intervenes when you least expect it. He will take you down paths that you are unprepared for emotionally and physically. As for me, this book has been a journey of unforgettable and beautiful moments. Some moments have been like shooting stars streaking across a cold, dark, winter sky, and other moments have been warm and soft like the embers in a fireplace on Christmas Eve. These are the moments that have touched my soul and will stay with me forever. Because as we all know, true love never dies.

Hope to see you down at the shore sometime,

Samantha

CPSIA information can be obtained
at www.ICGtesting.com
Printed in the USA
BVHW030950080322
630902BV00013B/487/J